SERGEANT CLUFF
STANDS FIRM

SERGEANT CLUFF STANDS FIRM

GIL NORTH

With an Introduction by
MARTIN EDWARDS

This edition published 2016 by
The British Library
96 Euston Road
London
NW1 2DB

Originally published in 1960 by Chapman & Hall Ltd

Cataloguing in Publication Data

A catalogue record for this book is
available from the British Library

ISBN 978 0 7123 5646 6

Typeset by Tetragon, London
Printed and bound by
TJ International Ltd, Padstow, PL28 8RW

INTRODUCTION

Sergeant Cluff Stands Firm launched a series featuring a Yorkshire detective which eventually ran to eleven novels. Not only did the books enjoy considerable popularity, but the eponymous sergeant also became a television detective, brought vividly to life by Leslie Sands. Despite this success, rather more than half a century after Cluff's first appearance in print, he has become a forgotten detective. Yet as this book shows, he is a distinctive and impressive character, and the crisp, concisely written stories about him retain their power to this day.

Cluff's first recorded case concerns the death of a woman in her forties. Amy Wright had married late in life, to a much younger man. She was quite comfortably off, yet is found dead at her home, poisoned by gas in her own bedroom. The local coroner presides over the inquest—splendidly described—which reaches the predictable verdict that Amy has committed suicide while the balance of her mind was disturbed. Modern readers may better appreciate the nuances of local reaction to Amy's death if they bear in mind that, when this novel first appeared, suicide was still a crime in the UK; decriminalization only came with the Suicide Act 1961.

One person is not satisfied, and that is Sergeant Caleb Cluff. Cluff lives alone in an old cottage in his native Gunnarshaw, with a dog, a cat, and an irascible cleaning lady for company. He comes from farming stock, and his brother, who farms at nearby Cluff End, plays an important part in the story. Cluff has never married, but possesses a deep understanding of human nature, born of years of observing life in a small community at close quarters; in this respect, if in no others, he resembles Agatha Christie's Miss Marple.

Like so many fictional detectives, Cluff has a difficult relationship with those in authority, and in particular with the officious Inspector Mole, who resents feeling much less at ease with the local community than his stubborn, taciturn subordinate. At first glance, Cluff seems almost to be a caricature of the grumpy Yorkshireman, but beneath the dour, reticent exterior lurks an instinctive sympathy for the underdog, as well as a fierce contempt for arrogance and cruelty.

He commands the respect of young Constable Barker, who is a witness when Cluff menaces Amy's selfish and shallow husband, whom he suspects of being responsible—morally, if not legally—for Amy's death. Barker does not, however, have the temerity to voice his private thoughts about Cluff: "... the most down-to-earth of all of us. Your feet on the ground, rooted in the soil. Everything about you—what people mean when they talk of the countryman ... Unshakable." In this story, Cluff behaves like an avenging angel, determined to seek justice for Amy Wright, and allowing nothing and no one to stand in his way.

It is almost a cliché to compare a strongly evoked setting for a crime novel to a character in the story, but it is undoubtedly true that the sturdy market town of Gunnarshaw, and the bleak, rain-swept moorland outside its boundaries, combine to form the perfect complement to Cluff's dogged personality. The dead woman's husband soon becomes overwhelmed by a claustrophobia induced partly by conscience:

> The smallness of Gunnarshaw, the knowledge of its people about each other, oppressed him. He felt suddenly that there was nowhere in Gunnarshaw he could turn, that Sergeant Cluff, if he was not around the first corner, must always be waiting round the second.

The storyline is strong, but this is not a whodunnit; Gil North's focus is not on mystification for the sake of game-playing, but on the human condition. His work shows the influence of Georges Simenon, and his most famous character, Inspector Jules Maigret. Nor is North unique as a British disciple of Simenon, who also inspired two other novelists working at much the same time as North. They also had their books televised, although long after *Cluff* reached the screens; Alan Hunter was the author of the novels adapted for the screen as *Inspector George Gently*, while the Cornishman W.J. Burley was the creator of *Wycliffe*.

Gil North was the pen-name of Geoffrey Horne (1916–1988), who was born in Skipton, where his father was the Town Clerk. After attending the local grammar school, where he became head boy, he studied at Christ's College, Cambridge. He took a double First, and also acquired a diploma in social anthropology. Joining the Colonial Service, he spent many years in Nigeria and the then British Cameroon.

As a "bush" district officer, in charge of areas of up to 5,000 square miles in size, he found that the experience of boyhood holidays on a hill-farm in the Dales helped him to bond with the local farmers and fishermen. He described his job in Africa as that of a jack-of-all trades: "magistrate, coroner, officer-in-charge of divisional police detachments, divisional prison officer and sub-Treasurer". He retired in the mid-fifties as the wind of change blew through Africa, and returned to Skipton—where *Cluff* was filmed, and on which Gunnarshaw is based—determined to pursue his interest in writing.

At first, he wrote under his own name, producing novels such as *No Escape*, which drew on his knowledge of Africa; a children's book about pirates set in the Caribbean, *Quest for Gold*, which he dedicated to his son Josh; and short stories. He digressed into detective fiction mainly as a means of "relaxation", but once he found he could make crime pay, Sergeant Cluff began to monopolize his attention.

He continued to write about Cluff long after the television series came to an end in 1965. In all there were eleven Cluff novels, all written in his characteristically staccato style, together with a handful of short stories. For a very different book, *A Corpse for Kofi Katt*, published in 1978, he returned to Africa for fictional inspiration. Kofi Katt, the son of a wealthy English father and a black mother, is a police superintendent with a social conscience who investigates the death of a nameless beggar whose body is found trapped in the mangroves. Katt may have been envisaged as an interesting new series character, but the book had no successors.

The author's son Josh Horne thinks it fair to say that there was a good deal of his father in Cluff. The author may have studied at Cambridge, and worked for many years in foreign parts, but he remained at heart a stolid Dalesman, strongly conservative in his outlook. During the Swinging Sixties, he was content to label himself as "the squarest of squares, hotly opposed to the new permissive society [and] its lack of discipline". Yet there is an even more striking characteristic of Sergeant Cluff that stands out, in this book, and elsewhere in the series. He is, beneath that formidable exterior, unquestionably a man of genuine compassion.

MARTIN EDWARDS
www.martinedwardsbooks.com

CHAPTER I

S ILENT IN THE OLD COTTAGE ISOLATED AT THE FOOT OF THE moors. Silent except for the crackling of the log fire in the grate, or a sudden flurry of rain beating against the windows, or a more pronounced moan from the wind hurtling over the moor tops.

The silence shattered. The harsh ringing of a telephone, regular, unceasing.

The dog in front of the fire stirred and rumbled in his throat. In the passage outside the living-room the telephone continued its strident summons.

The dog was big, shaggy, of a working breed, descended from a line of collies. He climbed to his feet, his gaze shifting to his master, nodding in a large arm-chair, comfortable, at peace.

The dog began to bark. The man in the chair jerked, coming to life. A cat, built on the same generous proportions as the dog, slept on the man's knees. Everything alive in the cottage was huge in the dancing shadows cast by the fire and the dim light of the single oil-lamp, turned low. The long fur of the cat, grey, Persian, stood on end. The cat's claws unsheathed and dug through the cloth of the man's trousers, into his thigh.

"Quiet, Clive! Quiet!" the man ordered.

He heaved his bulk reluctantly from the chair, holding the cat. The cat protested, its protests dying as the man placed it in the warm hollow of the cushion on which he had been sitting.

The dog's tongue lolled from his open jaws. His flanks rose and fell. His alert eyes followed the man as the man moved slowly, deliberately, without haste, to the passage.

"Yes?" said the man into the mouthpiece of the telephone. "Of course. Cluff speaking."

His words dropped like stones into a pool, broad-vowelled, well spaced, with long pauses between them.

"What?" he said. "Where? Number thirty-three, Balaclava Street? I suppose so. Not long. Half-an-hour. No more. Less."

The cat did not move.

"Stay, Clive! Sit!" Cluff said.

The dog sank to his haunches. The dog's ears pricked as the outer door slammed. The dog's head inclined lower in disappointment as a car engine started with difficulty, wheezing and clanking.

Rain plastered itself against the yellowed windscreen of the bull-nosed, two-seater Morris, defeating the efforts of the worn wipers. The ancient car travelled the dark road, freewheeling into a deep dip, labouring up the opposite hill at snail's pace. The steering wheel twisted in Cluff's loose grip. Cluff's heavy tweeds were damp and redolent in the confined space under the tattered hood. His shapeless tweed hat, with the grouse feather in its band, hooded his eyes. On the seat beside him the handle of a thick, chestnut-wood walking-stick, its ferrule wedged against the gear lever, bounced with every jolt.

The lights of houses ahead. The main road into Gunnarshaw. The car knew its own way. Down to the church. The High Street. At the bottom of the High Street, left. Past shuttered shops. The glare of a hotel. Right, into Little Crimea.

Sevastopol Road. The car slowed. Side-streets ran away from the road, at right-angles to it, climbing a hill. Between the mouths of the streets rows of houses, opening directly on to the pavement, all alike, a door, a parlour window, the windows upstairs of a larger bedroom and a smaller one. Sometimes the glass in these smaller windows was frosted, where the room behind had been turned from its original purpose into a bathroom. The curtains in the light of the infrequent street-lamps were white, neat and clean, the doorsteps scrubbed and holystoned.

Inkerman Street. Alma Street. Scutari Street.

Cluff crouched forward, staring into the night. A grocer's on one corner. A cobbler's on the other. He swung the wheel, regardless of whether there was traffic behind him, disdaining the use of an indicator, sidling like a crab into Balaclava Street. The street was unadopted and the rear wheels of the car spun on the slope slippery with the rain, scouring the wet grass, sending mud flying. Cluff pulled on the brake. He climbed out and the car ran backwards a little, until chocked by a boulder.

He could feel it in the blackness, a difference in atmosphere, a sense of evil, of things hidden. The doors he passed should have been locked and bolted. In the dark they appeared closed, but Cluff had an impression that they were open, just the slightest of cracks, people listening behind them in unlit hallways. Pale patches showed in the upstairs windows of the houses on the side opposite to him, disappearing when he paused to look. Eyes watched him. More than once he heard a quick intake of breath. At the top of the hill a dog escaped. Someone shouted and a short, staccato yelp of pain came to Cluff's ears.

Three quarters of the way up light spilled from an open door on to the flagged pavement. Heavy-shod feet clattered towards him. A uniformed constable almost knocked Cluff down.

"There, Sergeant," the constable said, turning to point. "Up there."

A smallish man, stocky, with a permanently hostile manner, dressed in Inspector's uniform, hopped about in front of the open door.

"At last, Sergeant," the Inspector said. "Do we have to wait all night?"

Cluff ignored him.

Inspector Mole, dripping, angry to be called out on such a night, grew more irritated, conscious of Cluff's physical mastery. Liberty of action amongst his inferiors offended him. Unorthodoxy was anathema to him. He was a natural man, suitably married, the father of a family. He conducted himself with decorum in all his actions, official and unofficial. He had a tidy mind and Caleb Cluff with his dog and his cat and his cottage two miles from town, fitted into none of his pigeon-holes. He supposed that one representative of the County Criminal Investigation Department was essential in the division. He was at a loss to understand how the Sergeant had made the plain clothes branch in the first instance.

Behind Mole, in the doorway out of the rain, a little woman could not keep still. She was thin and angular, dried-up, with peaked features, wispy grey hair, a long nose, a receding chin. She wore cotton stockings under her crumpled skirt and her jumper was of a neutral colour. Her watery eyes stared past Mole at Cluff, through black-rimmed glasses fixed to her ears by metal sidepieces. A man without a jacket, his waistcoat unbuttoned, his collar and tie discarded, fat overlapping the belt holding his trousers up, leaned unperturbed against a passage wall.

"Well?" asked Cluff. "Well?"

"Next door—" Inspector Mole began.

"It's all nonsense," the man interrupted. "I told her so. She's got you out for nothing."

"Don't listen to him, Sergeant," the woman pleaded. "If the sky fell on him he wouldn't notice. I know there's something wrong. I know it!"

"Tell me about it, Mrs. Toogood," Cluff said, quietly.

"Damn him!" Mole swore to himself. "How does he come to know everybody in Gunnarshaw? What chance have the rest of us got?"

"I always said so," the woman went on, in a piercing voice. "Married. At forty-five. To him. Twenty years younger, if he's a day!"

"Look," said her husband. "Why don't you come in? She'll talk for hours."

"Amy?" Cluff asked. "Is it Amy?"

"The milk," Mrs. Toogood said. "It hasn't been taken in. On the back doorstep. The paper, sticking through the front letter-box. I haven't heard anything all day. There's no light."

"Gone out," said Mr. Toogood. "She doesn't have to account to you for her movements."

Cluff moved forward. "I'll take this way," he said. "It's quicker than going round the row."

Mole and the constable followed him through the house. Its owners tagged on to the end of the procession. Cluff led them into the backyard, out into the back-street, into the yard of the house next door.

"You can see for yourselves," Mrs. Toogood said. "The curtains, still over the window—"

CHAPTER II

"THOMAS!" CLUFF SAID TO THE POLICE-CONSTABLE. "Break it in."

Constable Thomas drew himself up. He spat on his hands and rubbed them together. Then he took the doorknob in his fingers and pulled and pushed without effect.

"I don't like it," Inspector Mole told Cluff. "After all, there may be a perfectly reasonable explanation. The Superintendent—"

Constable Thomas retreated as far as the yard would let him. He charged at the back door, sideways, with all the force of his sixteen stones. Something cracked and the wood of the jamb splintered.

"Ah," said the constable.

He tried again and the door burst open.

"My God!" Mole exclaimed. "My God!"

Mrs. Toogood screamed, holding her hands to her nose.

Sergeant Cluff looked about him. A tiny rockery occupied the corner of the yard wall and the house side. Cluff picked up one of the rocks and hurled it through the ground-floor window.

Gas flooded out into the night.

"Take her home," Cluff told Mr. Toogood. "Go on. Take her home."

Mr. Toogood laid his hand on his wife's arm. He led her away and she was unwilling to go.

"What did I tell you?" Mrs. Toogood sobbed. "Didn't I say all along?—"

They waited in the yard. Voices hummed about them, people moving in and out of their houses in the night.

Cluff put his handkerchief over his mouth and nostrils. He blundered into the scullery, out of it into the living-room, from there to the passage. He groped for the lock on the front door. He found it and pulled the door open, taking gulps of pure air, while a draught surged past him. The lower floor cleared gradually of gas, but it was thick on the stairs, slow in dispersing.

Cluff went back to the yard.

"You can come in now," he said to Mole.

"Thank you," the Inspector replied, with sarcasm. "It's kind of you to invite me." He turned to the constable. "Keep people out down here, Thomas," he ordered.

Cluff was at the bottom of the stairs. He pressed a light-switch and mounted quickly. The three doors on the landing were all closed. Cluff pushed open the one nearest to the stairhead and knew at once that he had found the source of the gas. He stumbled across the room in the light shining from the landing and got the curtains drawn back and the window up. He leaned dizzily over the sill. His brain cleared and he could hear a tiny, hissing sound.

Cluff staggered back to the door and put the light on. A pipe, bent at the top, with a tap on its arm, stuck through the floor on the hearth of the fireplace. Cluff twisted the tap with his fingers and it moved stiffly. The hissing stopped.

"Are you all right?" Mole said, from the landing.

Mole stared about him at a room like hundreds of other rooms in Gunnarshaw. In the corner, a fireplace, its grate, which had probably never held a fire since the house was built, black-leaded. A double-bed, for which there was just space, was squashed close to the fireplace. An upright chair stood on one side of the bed. At the foot of the bed, hardly separated from it, a dressing-table. A wardrobe by the window. The wallpaper had a glaring, flowered design. Linoleum covered the floor, relieved by runners of carpet on either side of the bed and in front of the dressing-table.

Mole bent to look more carefully at the gas-tap. "They must have had a gas-fire once," he said.

Cluff was at the bed.

"Is she dead?" Mole asked. "It's lucky the window wasn't quite closed at the top and that the doors don't fit properly. The whole concern might have gone up."

On the side away from the fireplace the covers on the bed were smooth, flat. They were moulded into a hump where the body lay on the other edge. She was turned on her side, her hair long and silky, her face younger looking than Mole had expected. Her features were calm and compassionate. Mole decided they wore an expression of pity, as if she was sorry, not merely for herself, but for the world as well.

Her clothes were on the chair beside her head, a brassière dangling from the chair-back, a vest with shoulder-straps of pink ribbon, a slip, a pair of knickers, elastic round the waist and legs.

Mole's eyes wandered farther. A brush and comb lay on a glass tray on the dressing-table, together with a jar containing hair-grips. There was nothing else he could see except a lavender-bag, of faded blue velvet, hanging from one of the uprights of the mirror.

Mole said, "You'd have thought she would have left a note. But they don't always. What are you doing?" he added.

The Sergeant was folding back the bed-covers. He felt the dead woman's head gently with the tips of his fingers. She had on a nightdress of some thin stuff, not transparent, but not too thick to hide the shape of her breast. The point of her nipple pricked against the cloth.

"She doesn't look her age," Sergeant Cluff said.

"Nearly as old as me," Inspector Mole muttered. "Or you. Was she a friend of yours? Most people in Gunnarshaw seem to be."

"When you've been here as long as I have," Cluff said, "you'll know people like I do."

"It's not difficult," said the Inspector, "in a town this size."

"I was born not far away," Cluff said. "Even as a boy I used to come in with my father every market-day."

The Sergeant stooped over the bed, sniffing at the woman's mouth.

"Can't you leave that sort of thing to the doctor?" Mole demanded.

He watched Cluff turn the tap on the gas-pipe backwards and forwards.

"It wasn't turned on accidentally," Mole said.

"I was making sure," Cluff replied.

"She did it herself," Mole stated.

"Why?" Caleb Cluff asked. "Why?"

"How do I know why?" the Inspector exclaimed. "It's obvious, isn't it? It'll be something for you to find out, a nice change from petty thefts and amateur attempts at burglary. I can't see that it matters."

CHAPTER III

M OLE AND CLUFF WAITED FOR THE SURGEON. THEY KILLED time by going through the house together. The wardrobe in the bedroom held a man's suit and one of the drawers in the dressing-table contained a man's underwear, vests and pants and stockings, a couple of shirts.

"No children?" Mole asked.

"No," Cluff told him.

"She left it a bit late, didn't she?" Mole said.

The second bedroom, overlooking Balaclava Street, was furnished but sterile, as though no one ever slept in it. The bathroom into which the third bedroom had been converted offered nothing. Downstairs the front parlour smelt musty and showed no indication that it was ever used, unless on special occasions or at times such as Christmas.

In the living-room the rain blew through the smashed window. There were cold ashes in the grate. The room was clean, tidy, crockery stacked neatly away in the cupboards, everything as it should be, bearing the stamp of a careful housewife. Newspapers and some copies of a women's magazine were lumped together in a rack near the hearth. The mantelpiece held a clock and two vases. A handbag on the side-board contained a purse and a few oddments, a handkerchief, a folder with five one-pound notes and three ten-shilling ones.

"It's not often you find a woman who doesn't use powder and lipstick," Mole remarked, noting the lack of cosmetics.

"She wasn't any the worse for that," Cluff said.

"There's nothing to get excited about," Mole replied.

The police surgeon arrived. He made entries on a form he held in his hand.

The surgeon said, "Amy Wright. Born Snowden, you say?"

Cluff nodded.

"Married," the surgeon wrote. He paused. "Where's her husband then?"

Neither Cluff nor Mole enlightened him.

"Well," the surgeon said, "someone'll have to identify her formally. I can get the details later." He looked down his nose. "You can never tell," he said. "Especially at the menopause."

"You didn't know her," Cluff said.

The doctor closed his bag with a snap:

"She can be moved now, so far as I'm concerned. A foregone conclusion."

"The post-mortem?" Cluff said.

"Naturally. We have to go through the motions. Tomorrow, when I get the coroner's order."

The doctor laughed:

"There's nothing to worry about, Cluff. This case isn't going to get you promotion."

CHAPTER IV

CALEB CLUFF LAY ON HIS BACK, ARMS ON THE PILLOW BEHIND his head, staring at the sloping roof of his bedroom. Early winter light crept through the dormer window, which had a broad, cushioned sill. His bed was big, to accommodate his bigness. The counterpane rose in a hill over his large belly. The floor was of dark, oak boards, resting on the oak beams of the room beneath, strewn with sheepskin rugs, the fleeces intact. Books filled shelves fixed round the walls. When he turned his head he could see through the window pastures rising steeply to a plantation of firs. The cottage was too far from the road to be disturbed by the sound of traffic. The only noises he ever heard were the hoot of an owl, the shriek of a hare as a fox leapt on it, the cries of the peewits, the occasional far-off bleat of a sheep on the fells, his hens clucking in their run.

The sneck on his door rattled and lifted. His cat, whose name was Jenet, came leaping for his bed, clawing the covers, plumping its heavy body on his legs. Clive entered more sedately, one of a succession of Clives. The dogs on his father's farm had all been Clive and the bitches were always Lassie. The Sergeant was no less conservative than the rest of his family, no innovator, disinclined for change, a man who clung to the old ways. Clive squatted beside the bed and rested his head on its edge, gazing soulfully from brown eyes.

A tray descended on the bedside table. A brown teapot, a jug, a sugar-bowl, a cup and saucer stood on it. The woman who put it down was a woman of girth, with great cornucopias of breasts.

She waddled on short, sturdy legs. Her cheeks glowed, like Cluff's cheeks. She smelt of new milk and cream, of warm kitchens scented with fresh bread and baking cakes.

"Have you given up working?" the woman asked. "It's past eight."

Her name was Annie Croft. She came five mornings a week from the nearby hamlet to look after the cottage.

Cluff heard her feet on the wooden treads of the stairs. He sighed. He sat up and drank his tea, black and sweet. Clive's nose twitched at the smell of frying bacon.

The Sergeant got clumsily out of bed. His nightshirt billowed about him. He gazed into his mirror as he shaved. A round, strong-featured face, well jowled, with a bulldog look about it, gazed back. The crown of his head was bald. His dark hair, like a tonsure, was touched with silver. A determined nose jutted over tight lips.

He dressed. Jenet did not move from the place he had vacated in the bed. Clive trailed him downstairs, keeping close, but not importunate.

Cluff sat down in the chair by the fire, thoughtful, knowing his limitations. His hand stretched out to fondle the dog. He was grateful for the touch of Clive's tongue on his fingers.

"Aren't you going to eat it?" a voice asked.

Cluff looked up at Annie. His eyes wandered to the table where porridge steamed in a dish.

"You're not ill?" Annie demanded.

Cluff breakfasted. Jenet, chased from his bed by Annie, rushed spitting down the stairs to lay claim to the chair by the fire.

Cluff got out his car. Clive at his heels was quietly hopeful.

Annie put her head out of the upstairs window. She shouted:

"See you get to bed sooner tonight. You're too old to be gadding about at all hours."

Cluff stood by the car. He hated the car but he had to have it since he insisted on living so far from Gunnarshaw. He would rather have walked into the town, but it took too long. He put his hand on the car door. If the car was old he preferred age to youth. He felt more at home in the past than in the present.

He got into the car and sat there, not seeing anything. Clive stood in the porch, tense, his hopes fading. Suddenly Cluff whistled, galvanizing Clive into motion. The dog leapt for the seat beside the Sergeant and froze into stillness, afraid to be noticed again until the car was safely away.

Cluff stopped in the High Street. He took his walking-stick from the car. He told Clive:

"Stay!"

The High Street was wide, a ribbon of tar macadam, bordered on each side by a wide belt of stone setts between it and the pavements. Stalls, selling fruit and vegetables, were pitched here and there on the setts. There was little traffic and hardly any people moving about. The sky was heavy, close to the earth. The shop windows were lit up. A poster outside the entrance to a newsagent's shop screamed, in charcoal letters:

"Tragic death of Gunnarshaw woman."

At intervals along the lines of shops and offices and banks passages no wider than one man at a time could pass led off both sides of the High Street. They tunnelled the buildings and became tiny streets, cottages facing each other across gaps Cluff could have spanned with his arms extended. The W.C.s were separate at the ends of the rows of cottages and then the ginnels burrowed again under larger buildings before giving access to a road running parallel to the High Street.

Cluff, wearing an ancient Burberry swollen over his waist, his stick a third leg, turned into one of the ginnels. Many of the cottages were empty, condemned for demolition, their windows broken. Some had been converted into warehouses and storerooms. In one an optimist had established a moneylending business, unsuccessful because the people of Gunnarshaw never borrowed. At the far end two men were idling with hammers, pretending to break down a wall.

The words "Commission Agent" were painted in white on a window half-covered with sienna paint. Cluff pushed open the door beside the window without knocking, entering a cold, small room.

A fat man looked up from a newspaper spread on a desk and groped hurriedly for a pile of slips, which he stuffed into his trousers' pocket. He glanced at the Sergeant, grimacing sickly.

"Wright," Cluff said. "He runs for you. Where is he?"

"Not now," the fat man answered. "Not since you caught me last time. I only do business from the office now."

"Office!" repeated Caleb, gazing at the uncovered stone floor, spread with dirt, the peeling walls, the rusty fire-grate, the greasy brownstone sink into which a solitary tap wept slow tears.

"It's true," the bookmaker insisted.

"Wright," Cluff said again. "I want Wright."

"He doesn't work for me any more."

"Where is he?"

"Look," said the other. "I don't know anything. As God's my judge. It's here, in the Stop Press. His wife—"

"Tell me!"

"If I could. I'd let you know if I could. That man! I treated him well. He wasn't doing any business. He was setting up on his own when I thought he was working for me."

"Listen," Cluff said. "I'd see him for days together. Then there'd be a gap. He wouldn't be at any of his usual corners."

"Unreliable. I sacked him. He'd go off for two or three nights, nearly every week. On my money."

"Where?"

"I don't know."

"If you remember, get in touch with me."

The fat man got up. His chair rocked perilously. He grabbed at it to prevent it from falling. He thrust his hand into his pocket, stuffing his papers farther down.

"I wouldn't hold out on you, Sergeant," the fat man promised. "Try the caff across the street. He used to go in there a lot."

"Why don't you do some honest work?" the Sergeant said, as he went out.

"I'll try to find out for you," the fat man called eagerly. He wiped his brow with a soiled handkerchief. "I'll do what I can."

"That'll be the day," came the Sergeant's voice from the ginnel. "When you and me uphold the law together."

CHAPTER V

SERGEANT CLUFF EMERGED INTO THE HIGH STREET.
A woman sweeping the entrance to a shop said, "Caleb."

"Dolly," Sergeant Cluff replied.

He stood on the edge of the setts, looking across the road. Clive's nose pressed flat against the windscreen of his car. The Sergeant made a gesture at the dog. Clive dropped back on to the car seat.

Cluff crossed the road to a cheap transport café, its windows fly-blown. He went in. The café was narrow, stretching back from the street, a counter, stained with the droppings of food, down one side. Rickety stools faced the counter. A line of tables, without cloths, each supplied with a vinegar bottle and two metal shakers for salt and pepper, occupied the opposite wall.

There was a girl behind the counter. "What'll it be?—" she began.

She tossed back the mane of almost white hair that hung to her shoulders. Its roots on her forehead were darker, nearly black. She wore a tight sweater, moulding her breasts, which were low-slung in spite of their sponge supports. Her lips were red, matching her fingernails, but her face was greyish under its coating of powder. The folds on the skin of her neck, where the powder had not reached, showed traces of grime. Her hands were dirty. She watched Cluff through narrowed eyes, her nerves taut, backing against the shelves behind her. A newspaper lay on the counter. The girl let her eyes stray from the Sergeant to the paper and back again.

"Well?" Cluff said.

"Well what?" the girl demanded, with an effort at unconcern.

Her eyes were red with lack of sleep, black, sunken half-circles under them. Her clothes kept her flesh together and Cluff guessed that, undressed, she would be shapeless. He said nothing.

"What?" the girl asked. "What?"

"When did you see him last?"

"Who?"

"You know who."

"It's nothing to do with me. You can't blame me. I didn't even know he was married. Not," she added, sweetening the lie, "at first."

"Couldn't you find someone else to go to bed with?" Cluff asked.

"The bastard!" the girl said, wondering what she had escaped.

"When I was young," the Sergeant went on, "there weren't any women like you in Gunnarshaw."

"I have to live," the girl told him. "Don't imagine I'm fond of a dump like this."

"Get out!" said Cluff. "When this is over, get out. Or I'll put you somewhere you'll find less pleasant."

She looked into the street, through the glass panel in the door. She couldn't see anyone.

"I'll report you," the girl murmured. "I haven't done anything. You can't threaten me."

"Wait and see," Cluff said. "Where is he?"

"He hasn't been with me for weeks. You think I couldn't find a man better than him?"

"No money?" said Cluff.

"I could have had him if I'd wanted. What kind of a girl do you think I am?"

"I know what kind."

"He couldn't do without women. I can tell you that about him. I'm not surprised his wife wasn't enough."

"For some men a wife's never enough," Cluff said. "Did you know her?"

"Mutton dressed up as lamb," the girl said. "Cradle-snatcher! They never get past it, do they?"

"Careful," the Sergeant warned, leaning over the counter. "You couldn't hold a candle to her."

The girl's words tumbled over each other.

She said, "He came in here a lot when I first knew him and he never made a pass at me then. Come to think of it, I didn't see him with anyone else either."

She paused.

"It's funny," she continued. "After he got married, that's when it started."

In her excitement she leaned on the counter too. Cluff could smell the sourness of her breath. Her breasts were squeezed together on the wood and her flesh quivered above the neckline of her sweater.

The girl whispered, "I don't know where he went these last weeks. But he went somewhere. Not in Gunnarshaw. Somewhere else."

Cluff looked round the dingy café, his gorge rising at its staleness.

"A cup of tea?" the girl asked. "On the house."

"Remember what I said," Cluff told her. "Wherever you come from—get back there."

She watched him leave and he almost collided in the doorway with a young man in overalls, a cap on his head.

The young man said, "Have they caught up with you at last, Maisie?"

"I'm not afraid of him," Maisie replied. "Or of anybody like him."

"About tonight—" the young man murmured.

"You're the same as all the others," Maisie said, laughing.

At the police-station Inspector Mole said cleverly:

"I'm glad to see you, Cluff. It is Cluff, isn't it? Forgive me, but you're so much of a stranger here. So you've condescended to pay us a visit?"

"What do they allow him to live out in the country for?" Inspector Mole asked himself. "The fellow does as he likes."

The Inspector had only recently been promoted and transferred to Gunnarshaw. If the police division was large he considered the town itself too small for opportunity. He wasn't quite sure of his standing with his superiors and his uncertainty rankled.

"I should have joined a borough force," Mole thought. "It's a wonder I'm not still a village constable."

"Wright," said Cluff's voice, breaking into the Inspector's meditations. "Is there any news of Wright?"

To add to his other troubles Inspector Mole suffered both from indigestion and from a shrewish wife. "Let me see," he considered. "Oh yes, we had a death last night, didn't we?"

"What's the dog for?" the Inspector snapped. "To track Wright down with?"

Clive backed behind Cluff, snarling.

Mole, answering Cluff's question, said more quickly, "No, there isn't. He hasn't come back. At least, not when the man in Balaclava Street was last relieved."

Constable Barker was on the desk. Cluff came out of the Inspector's office, Clive close to him.

"Good dog," the constable said to Clive. "Good boy. Here then. Here!"

"I'm sorry, Sergeant," Barker said, stroking Clive's head. "I've seen you talking to her in the street. Did you know her well?"

"No more than anybody else," Cluff replied, gruffly.

"It's a shame," Barker said.

He was a young man, smooth-cheeked, with a big heart. He liked his fellow-men. He came from a happy home and he wasn't old enough yet to have lost his illusions.

"It doesn't seem right," Barker continued. "She could hardly have expected to get married at her age, but she did. What did she go and kill herself for?"

"Because she'd got married?" Cluff suggested.

"Surely not," Barker said. He was newly engaged himself. He added, "She'd everything to live for."

The Sergeant shook his head, despairing of understanding in Barker. He asked:

"Nothing in from the surgeon?"

"Not yet," Barker replied, his mind questing. "Of course it couldn't be murder. Not in Gunnarshaw. But what's happened to her husband?"

Inspector Mole's voice broke in from behind them:

"Don't be a fool, Barker. No more than you have to be."

The outer door closed behind Cluff.

Inspector Mole, addressing the room at large, stated flatly, "Sometimes I think he's off his rocker. I wish I had him under me. I'd show him a thing or two." He wrinkled his nose. "That damned dog of his! The place stinks."

"You wouldn't find a dog like that anywhere," Constable Barker said, in Clive's defence.

"That's the first sensible thing I've heard you say since I got here," Mole told Barker.

CHAPTER VI

"I T'S YOU AGAIN, IS IT?" MRS. TOOGOOD AT NUMBER THIRTY-one Balaclava Street said.

"Jack's working," Mrs. Toogood added. "She'd have been lying there yet if I'd listened to him. Aren't you coming in? Bring the dog. I don't mind dogs."

The door slammed to. Cluff went along the passage. He made himself comfortable in Mr. Toogood's chair. The rain ran down the window. He could see the backyard through the rain, a green-painted door to the lavatory, another green-painted door to the coal-place. The blank rear wall of number thirty-three's lavatory and coal-place divided its yard from this one. A low gate led into the back street. Across the street was another yard, identical in all respects.

"I'll make a cup of tea," Mrs. Toogood said from the scullery. "Your grandmother's dead, isn't she?"

"My grandmother?" Cluff repeated, surprised.

"When I was a lass," Mrs. Toogood said, "she'd a stall in the market on Saturdays. We used to buy butter and eggs from her. Old Mrs. Cluff of Cluff's Head."

"My brother John's got the farm now," Cluff said.

"Queer," commented Mrs. Toogood. "You always looked more of a farmer than he does. What did you join the police for?" She came into the room carrying a teapot. "Still," she said, "you're not so far off."

Mrs. Toogood reached over the Sergeant's shoulder to a cupboard in the wall.

"Don't move," she said. "I can manage."

She gave him a cup, filled to the brim.

"Just a minute. I'll find something for the dog," she said.

"Don't bother," Cluff told her.

"It's no bother."

She was disappearing back into the scullery:

"There's always some scraps left. I used to keep them for her dog."

Mrs. Toogood returned with a plate and put it on the floor in front of Clive.

"All right," Cluff said. "It's for you, Clive."

His hostess opened a tin and held it out.

"Have a biscuit," she invited. "Home-made."

She settled herself in a chair across the hearth from Cluff, cup and saucer in her hand.

"I don't mind telling you," she confided, "it's been a shock to me."

"I'd forgotten the dog," Cluff said. "Of course, she had one."

"Not everyone's cup of tea," Mrs. Toogood remarked, referring to Amy Wright's dog.

"A little dog," Cluff mused. "A terrier."

"Spoilt," Mrs. Toogood said. "You know how it is with old maids. A yapping, bad-tempered little beast. Not that I didn't get on with it. I did."

"A Yorkshire terrier."

"After she got married—" Mrs. Toogood said. "That dog hated him. It barked its head off every time he came in."

"You'd have thought it would have got used to him."

"Not it. They were at daggers drawn, those two. It bit him more than once. I've seen him put his foot to it when she wasn't looking."

"What happened to it?"

"She was heart-broken, poor thing. If she'd been sure, it would have been something. But she wasn't. It vanished a few days ago. Just like that. Into thin air."

"A dog she'd had for years? She treated it like a child."

"I wouldn't put it past him to have had something to do with it," Mrs. Toogood said, darkly.

Clive ate noisily. The fire roared up the chimney. It was hot in the room.

"You know," Mrs. Toogood said, "she's lived next door to me nearly all her life. We were close. She'd no one else to turn to, poor soul. An only child, left all on her own."

"I know," Cluff said.

"If she'd needed to work. If she'd been able to work. But after her father died there was her mother, bedridden, lingering on. When her mother went she was too old. It's tragic. She gave the best years of her life to her mother. She couldn't help it. She never had a chance to live like the rest of us."

"I know," Cluff repeated. "I know."

"I've thought about it, and thought," Mrs. Toogood said. "A mother shouldn't ask that of her daughter. Now look what's happened."

Clive, replete, put his head on the fender and stared at the blazing coals.

"You never get used to being alone," Mrs. Toogood said. "She couldn't stand it any longer."

Cluff twisted in his chair.

"She'd no experience," Mrs. Toogood said. "She couldn't see what he was. I tried to tell her, but it doesn't do to meddle. She didn't speak to me for weeks."

"There's no way to stop it," Cluff said.

"The older they are the harder they fall," Mrs. Toogood said. "Over forty and as innocent as a babe in arms. What did she know about men?"

The Sergeant was lost in thought. He gazed unblinking over Mrs. Toogood's head, his eyes fixed on a picture hanging on the wall.

Mrs. Toogood said, "That picture's hers. She was clever with her hands. She had to do something to fill in her time."

Cluff started. "It's good," he managed.

"She had money," Mrs. Toogood said. "Her father saw to that. He worked his fingers to the bone for her mother and her. He killed himself providing for them. The house was hers too."

"Yes," Cluff agreed.

"Wright knew about it," Mrs. Toogood said, wisely. "What else could he have been after?"

"He came from the south with a firm of builders," Cluff said. "He ought to have gone back with them when the job was over."

"Shiftless. Lazy," said Mrs. Toogood. "He was breaking her heart. I've sat here in the evenings and listened to him shouting at her. For all she replied he might have been talking to himself. She never said a single word against him. It would have done her good if she had."

"I thought as much," Cluff said.

He did not seem pleased to have his suspicions confirmed. He sounded disappointed and defeated.

He asked, "So you're not surprised?"

"No," Mrs. Toogood replied. "I'm not surprised at anything."

"I'm looking for Wright," Cluff said.

"It's three or four days since he was last here."

"You're sure?"

Mrs. Toogood nodded.

"I haven't been much help, have I?" she asked. "But then, what is there to help with?"

The Sergeant went back to the police-station.

"Barker," he said, "has anyone reported a dog missing?"

"When?"

"In the last couple of weeks."

Constable Barker searched his records.

"Nothing here, Sergeant. Gunnarshaw isn't big enough for a dog to get lost in."

CHAPTER VII

T HE MORTUARY WAS NEAR THE SLAUGHTERHOUSE. IT DIDN'T have a permanent keeper. A works' foreman employed by the Council looked after it in addition to his other duties.

Cluff drew up in front of the mortuary. A light shone through its open door into the gathering dusk. He got out of his car and went into an entrance hall separated by a partition from the rest of the building. A man sat on a wooden chair, huddled in an overcoat, with a scarf round his neck.

The man said, "It's perishing in here, Sergeant. I'm chilled to the marrow."

"Shut the door," Cluff suggested.

"Nay," the man said. "I reckon nowt of closed doors in a place like this."

Cluff continued into the main room. It was brilliantly lit with unshaded bulbs, windowless. Water ran in a steady stream from a stainless tap into a very white porcelain sink fixed against the wall. Shelves contained bottles. The smell of disinfectant was strong.

In the middle of the room, plenty of space all round it, a table, not of wood but of metal, was supported on a single, bright shaft. The shaft had wheels and levers so that the table could be raised or lowered, inclined this way or that. By the head of the table a smaller table held an array of knives and scalpels.

The police surgeon, in a white coat splashed with spots of brown and stained in a larger patch where he had been bending, looked round when he heard Cluff come in. He moved aside.

Amy Wright lay on the table, stark-naked. She seemed smaller to Cluff than when he had known her in life. He remembered meeting her in the streets, a little dowdy, her clothes unfashionable, her hair arranged in an out-of-date style. He remembered stopping and passing the time of day with her. He could see now the heightened colour on her face, feel again her uncertainty, hear her quick words, slurred together in her nervousness.

He thought, "I understood. I could have done something about it. I wanted to."

He stared and stared. The surgeon looked at him.

Finally the surgeon said, "She can't complain now if you want to get an eyeful."

"Weren't there any other men in Gunnarshaw besides Wright?" Cluff thought.

The surgeon coughed. Cluff stood quite still. He could hear the movements of the man he had spoken to in the entrance.

The surgeon took a step forward.

"I see the waste too," the surgeon said. "I know as well as you do she couldn't have had much of a life. I know, like you do, she'll never have any compensation now, no reward for the past, no consolation, nothing to balance one side of her life against the other."

"She loved children," Cluff said. "I've seen her leaning over prams pushed by mothers she knew, and the expression on her face—"

"She was past childbearing," the surgeon said. "You can't make anything of it, Sergeant. There's nothing to be made of it. Nothing except that she released the gas and lay down on the bed and closed her eyes."

"I can't believe it," Cluff said.

"You have to believe it. I've finished with her. What's left can be buried and forgotten. No one drugged her and left her on the bed. No one battered her into unconsciousness. There's nothing in her stomach but the remains of her last meal. There's nothing in her blood except what I knew there would be. She hasn't a bruise or a mark from head to toe that's of any significance. I've looked in her mouth and in her nostrils. I've examined her lungs. I know how she died. She died exactly as it appeared to Mole and you last night."

"Still—" Cluff began.

"Even a suicide's unusual in this town," the surgeon continued. "But don't let it get you down. Was it murder you hoped for, so that you could take the revenge she can't take? She died by her own hand and you'll have to let it rest there. That's where you must leave it, Cluff."

"Good night," the Sergeant said.

He sat in his car. It was almost dark. The mills were emptying. Men and women flowed in a steady stream along the pavements, their shoes clattering, their voices raised.

The street was empty again. Lamplight shone on the road. Clive huddled close to him. The night was cold, the rain stopped. A star showed through a gap in the clouds, which were drifting gently, breaking into wisps and rags. There was a hint of frost in the air.

Cluff twisted the ignition key and tapped his foot on the accelerator. He depressed the clutch and put the car in gear. He released the brake and allowed the pedal to rise slowly from the floor. He drove towards the High Street, along which he had to go to reach his cottage.

Out of the corner of his eye Cluff saw a man looking into the window of a shoe-shop, his back to the roadway, his shoulders hunched, his hands dug deep into his pockets. The car halted with a jerk, throwing Clive against the dashboard. Cluff looked out, one arm thrust through the sidescreen, ready to beckon, his mouth open to shout. The man turned away from the shop and walked off. It wasn't Wright.

The clock in the church tower at the top of the High Street struck six. The lights in the window of the shoe-shop went out. Two girls tapped past, arm-in-arm, laughing, talking animatedly. Their lips were reddened and their faces powdered, their clothes tight about their young bodies. They disappeared along the street, out of sight round a corner. A louder outburst of their voices floated back to Cluff.

He started the car once more. He backed and turned. He followed the street into a wider road, away from the direction he had originally intended. The lamp-posts were farther apart. There was a break in the buildings where the road bulged into a semicircular cobbled expanse. He followed the edge of the half-circle to where a stone arch gave entrance to a dimly-lit tunnel.

Through the arch an iron grille blocked the other end of the tunnel. Beyond the grille was a platform and, across two railway tracks, another with a square box of a waiting-room on it. Cluff went into a wooden-floored hall to his right, the pigeon-holes of a ticket-office on one side of him, a barrier on the other.

A sort of box stood by the barrier. A man in uniform sat in the box, his head nodding forward on to his chest. A face bent to one of the pigeon-holes, looked through it, and vanished. The man in the box opened his eyes at the sound of Cluff's feet and leaned out. Down the line an engine whistled, coming nearer.

"Sergeant," the ticket-collector said, peering more closely at Cluff.

"A man," Cluff said, "a thin, dark-haired man, clean-shaven, white-faced. About five foot six. Nine stone maybe. In his twenties. A man who might travel, say, once a week, or once in two weeks, staying away for a night or two."

The collector scratched his chin.

"By train perhaps," Cluff added. "Or by bus. I don't know."

The collector lifted a newspaper lying on a shelf beside him. He prodded the paper with his finger.

The collector said, "It's all in here. I saw it this morning. But they've got the full story now."

A goods train rattled through the station, its engine spitting steam.

"Not while I've been on duty," the collector said. He was silent for a moment. "I saw her the other evening. I live close to Balaclava Street, you know."

"Yes, you do," the Sergeant said.

"It wasn't dark. Not quite dark. I've an allotment over the canal. I was hurrying to get a few sprouts. She was going along the canal bank. I didn't think then I wouldn't see her again."

"The canal bank?" Cluff asked. "The towpath's full of holes, slippery with mud. She was fastidious, her shoes always spotless."

"I asked her, 'What are you doing here?' It was near the swing bridge. She said, 'I'm looking for Scruffy. I can't find him.' 'If he'd got into the canal, Amy,' I said, 'he'd be able to get out. There's plenty of places where the banks are crumbling. I saw a cow fall in last week and it got out. What a cow can do a dog can.' I said, 'And that terrier of yours is wick. I've never seen a dog so wick.' 'He's never gone off before,' she said. 'Don't worry,' I said. 'You'll find him. Perhaps he's gone back home. He might be waiting for you.' 'Yes,' she said. 'Probably you're right. I'll go and see.'"

They were silent, thinking.

Cluff drove aimlessly. He looked out of the car and recognized Sevastopol Road. He wondered what he was doing back in this part of the town. He stopped and walked up Balaclava Street. Number thirty-three was dark and apparently deserted.

He continued along Sevastopol Road. He came to its end and crossed another road at right-angles to it. He climbed a short slope and saw in his headlights a wooden bridge, a platform with hand-rails and a balk of timber as a handle to swing it open.

The canal was still and murky, black, evil-smelling. Cluff followed Clive along the towpath. The engine-house of a mill bordered the bank, shutters closing off the coal bunkers. Coal dropped from the grab of a crane in its transfer from barge to mill crunched as Cluff stepped on it. The crane itself, four-wheeled, its cab above him in the air, its jib protruding, loomed in the dark. He stumbled over Clive, who had a leg lifted against one of the wheels.

The Sergeant's eyes became accustomed to the night. The sky had cleared more since his visit to the railway-station. Now that he was out of range of his car lights the canal was not so much obscured. Empty tins and half-submerged bottles floated in the water. An abandoned motor-tyre, on edge, two-thirds sunk, arched above the surface.

"Clive," Cluff called. "Clive!"

Down the path the dog whined and scratched.

"Clive," Cluff shouted again.

He walked quickly. Water splashed cold on his ankles as he put a foot into a deep puddle. Clive, forelegs bent, scrabbled with his paws at an anonymous mass, swollen, bloated, sodden.

"Come away, Clive," Cluff ordered.

He stopped. He could make out a canvas sack, stranded in weeds overhanging the water where the bankside had collapsed. He took Clive by the scruff of the neck, pulling him back. Clive struggled to get free, obsessed with the sack.

Cluff released the dog. He spoke sharply and Clive squatted, quivering. The Sergeant looked up and down the canal. He could see the bridge in the direction from which he'd come. Beyond him on the other side the canal stretched away straight and calm. The sky was studded with stars and a moon was rising. The water reflected the stars.

He grabbed at the sack. It collapsed when he touched it with a soft hiss. He tried again, ignoring the slime he felt on his palms. He steeled himself. He went down on his knees, clutching with both hands. Water ran up his sleeves.

He flung another admonition at the trembling dog. He unbuttoned his overcoat, which was wet where he had had to hug the sack to get it on to firm ground. He felt in his trousers' pocket for a penknife. The sack was like a balloon.

Cluff slashed the string round the neck of the sack. He held his breath, trying to close his nostrils to the stench. The sack stuck to its contents.

He felt in his pocket again, for matches this time. He wiped his hands on his coat. He cupped them carefully, shielding the flame, nursing it until the matchstick caught fire. The match went out, but he had seen enough.

He rubbed his hands a second time down the front of his coat. He could not rid them of putrefaction. He filled his pipe and lit it, and he thought he could taste decay. He stood on one leg and knocked his pipe out against the boot of his other foot before thrusting the pipe back into his pocket.

Cluff stayed there for a long time. Where the mill wall ended grass grew long against a railing, encroaching on the bank.

He took the sack and hid it in the grass.

CHAPTER VIII

THE CONSTABLE ON BEAT DUTY SAW THE CAR ON THE SLOPE leading up to the canal. He stood thinking, "A courting couple." He couldn't make up his mind whether to go to the car and move it on or not. He told himself, "Damn it! Where else can they go?" He remembered that he had a daughter of his own and it occurred to him that he wouldn't like her to be in a stationary car at night with a man.

The constable stalked up the slope. The bridge was white in the moonlight. A figure perched on the wooden rail, motionless, immense, its head inclined. A dog sat on the bridge deck, just as still.

The constable recognized the car. He quickened his pace and passed it.

"Sergeant," the constable said, raising his voice. "Sergeant!"

Cluff moved slightly.

"They're looking for you at the station," the constable said, apologetically. "They've been looking all over for you."

"I've been trying to get you on the phone, Sergeant," Barker told Cluff later. "We were sure you'd gone home. I couldn't get any reply from the cottage."

Barker gazed at the wet stain on Cluff's coat. He sniffed and looked at Clive and thought, "Perhaps Mole was right after all, but I've never smelt the dog before."

Aloud Barker said, "In there," pointing to a door in the wall beyond his desk.

The room was colder because of its appearance. The walls were painted in a dark shade of green, glossy with varnish. The floor was covered with linoleum, as frigid and repellent as the walls. A table, of plain wood, with a straight, wooden chair behind it, stood lost and mournful in empty space. The only other furniture was a couch, horsehair, a Victorian antique, thrust crosswise in the far corner.

The light was harsh. A high-powered bulb hung under a flat china shade shaped like a plate. The only shadow in the room was a circle on the ceiling, immediately above the shade. It was pale, grey, hardly worth calling a shadow.

Sergeant Cluff stopped in the doorway. The occupant of the couch lifted his head and their eyes met. They stared at each other.

The Sergeant closed the door. He marched ponderously to the chair behind the table and sat down, unfastening his coat but keeping his hat on his head. Clive stretched under the table, muzzle between his forepaws, watching the couch.

The man on the couch shivered. His face was colourless. He grinned, without mirth, in a purely nervous reaction. His features contorted.

Cluff's eyes narrowed. They were piercing beneath lowered lids. The natural redness of his cheeks turned into a brick colour and spread down his neck to his shirt collar, which looked tight and constricting. He breathed deeply, his chest rising and falling. His fists clenched and he held himself in with an effort, willing himself to stay seated.

The visitor squirmed. The cloth of his trousers' seat scraped on the horsehair roughness of the couch. A stray lock of lank hair hung over his forehead, above his right eye. He was meagre under his gabardine raincoat, his knees pointed, his shanks like sticks under their covering. His eyes were shifty, never still. His lips were hardly perceptible. His nose was sharp, like a ferret's. He gave the impression of being suddenly trapped. He opened his mouth. His teeth were needles.

In the outer office Barker fidgeted. The round clock on the wall ticked, the movement of its black fingers visible.

At the table Cluff relaxed. He sank into a torpor, only his eyes alive. The eyes of his victim darted from corner to corner, resting for longer and longer on the door. His victim considered, not consciously but by instinct, making a break for it, a desperate rush to escape. He could not endure the quiet, the inaction, the accusation with which the whole atmosphere of the room was pregnant. The dog never took its gaze off him and he was worried by the dog. The dog's jowls were drawn back, showing the dog's fangs. The man the dog was watching was certain that the dog would spring into life at any moment and jump for his throat. He could not hold his hands steady. He had to press them hard on his thighs to conceal their trembling. A pulse began to beat at the side of his jaw.

Barker, turned to the closed door, cocked his ears. He was afraid, but he did not know of what.

On the couch the man put his hand in his coat pocket. He snatched a newspaper from the pocket, tearing it in his haste. He held it out and the paper shook. It was dog-eared, dirty, folded and folded again, rolled into a baton.

The man stammered, "I didn't know until I saw the paper—"

"You!" Cluff said, after a long pause. "You!"

Silence settled between them again.

Wright's voice was a scream, high-pitched. It made Constable Barker jump at his desk.

"They told me to wait for you," Wright wailed. "I'm here. I'm waiting. What do you want to do with me?"

"She's dead," Cluff said. "Dead! Dead!"

Wright buried his face in his hands.

Wright's shoulders heaved. He lost what little power of controlling his limbs remained to him. A hand seized him by the hair. His head was jerked up, his face thrown back. Cluff glared down at him.

"Crying won't help," Cluff said.

The hate in the words, the contempt, the violence of Cluff's anger was like a douche of icy water, swilling Wright, holding him speechless. He shrank away and his head was free. Cluff's arm was like a club raised to strike him.

Barker opened the door:

"Sergeant!"

Barker called again, urgently, "Sergeant!"

Cluff's hand dropped slowly. Cluff turned.

"Get back to your desk," Cluff said. "Get back! Do you hear me?"

"No," Wright yelled. "No! Don't leave me here with him. Don't! Don't! Don't!"

Barker stood stupefied. Cluff walked back to his chair.

"Leave the door open if you like," Cluff said.

"Leave it open," Cluff repeated. "Let some air in here."

"Now," Cluff said to Wright. "Now. Tell me the story you've made up. Tell me the lies you came to tell me."

Wright could see Barker through the open door. Barker's presence made him bolder.

"What's the use?" Wright demanded, but indistinctly. "I'll say nothing. Not to you. You wouldn't believe me if I did."

"Barker," Cluff shouted. "Barker!"

Barker leapt to his feet. Cluff marched through his office.

"Let him write it down if he wants to write it down," Cluff said. "Let Mole talk to him. Mole will believe him. Mole knows what's happened. There's no arguing with Mole."

"Clive!" Cluff said.

He walked out, followed by the dog. A self-starter whined. A car began to move. A horn barked, struck viciously, as the car bounded from the police-station and turned across the road.

Constable Barker put his hand to his head and wiped away the sweat.

"What did you say to him?" Barker asked Wright. "How did you get him like that?"

Wright's voice was a whimper.

"Nothing," Wright insisted. "I said nothing. He never so much as let me begin."

Wright's eyes took in Barker, from head to feet and back again. He saw that Barker was young.

"I want to see someone," Wright said. "An Inspector. A Superintendent. I want to complain."

"Not tonight," Barker said firmly. "Tomorrow. Come back tomorrow."

"I shan't run away," Wright said. "I've nothing to run away for. You saw what happened tonight. You're my witness."

"I saw nothing," Barker said. "There's no one here except you and me."

CHAPTER IX

THE TOWN HALL WAS NOT VERY BIG, AN OBLONG ROOM, with windows down one of its longer sides. The floor was smooth, polished for dancing in winter. The Council provided a stage at the far end for concerts and for amateur dramatic productions.

A movable witness box and a clerk's table were arranged in front of the stage. There was another table, and a chair, on the stage itself. Rows of chairs occupied the body of the hall. Representatives of the local press and witnesses sat in those nearest the stage. Only a few other persons were present.

The coroner entered from the dressing-rooms behind the stage. He enthroned himself above the common folk. A pimply youth laid a big book, with a dark red cover, on the table in front of him. The coroner was a little man, wearing pince-nez spectacles. He poured water from a carafe into a glass and sipped delicately. He put the glass down and rapped on the table with his knuckles. A constable brought the court to order.

Steam-heating made the atmosphere warm. A film of condensation dimmed the windows. Everything in the hall took place at a pace slower than that in the town outside, in a minor key, with a proper respect for the dead.

The people were as quiet as if they were attending a funeral service in church. They were as still as mice when a cat is about. They did not wriggle in their chairs. If they forgot themselves and moved they pulled themselves up sharply and glanced at their neighbours, embarrassed and ashamed. They suppressed their coughs, growing red in their faces. Those with colds dared only the tiniest of sniffs, tortured on the rack of respectability.

They were all dressed for the occasion, to avoid criticism, either from the public in general or from the coroner. Mrs. Toogood was erect in her Sunday best. Wright wore a dark suit, but he was no less ferrety than he had been at the police-station. If he expected anyone to be sorry for him he hoped in vain.

The coroner turned over the police reports. He looked at Wright with ill-concealed hostility. He sat without a jury and he was well aware of the extent of his powers and of the latitude allowed by his office. He was a Gunnarshaw man, one of a family that had conducted legal business in the town for generations and that would continue to do so for generations more. He was removable by death or old age or at his own wish. If he wanted to do a thing he did it, regardless of all the authorities in the land. As a coroner he was not overworked. He rarely had the pleasure of conducting an inquiry into a death of this nature. If he did not know the deceased well, at least he knew her by sight. They all did.

Mrs. Toogood clutched the rail of the witness box. She kept her eyes on Wright.

She said, "Of course she had. She'd plenty of reason. She was married to him, wasn't she? Wouldn't you have been worried? The house shut up. The doors locked."

"Answer my questions," the coroner told her. But he was pleasant about it, his manner mild. "When did you see her last? How did she appear to you then?"

"The day before," Mrs. Toogood replied. "In the afternoon. She'd been out shopping, I think. She was upset about her dog."

"Her dog?"

"Someone knows more about that than he'll admit," Mrs. Toogood affirmed, regarding Wright closely. "And about her being alone in the house. All alone. Without her dog."

"Indeed," said the coroner. He too stared at Wright.

Mole replaced Mrs. Toogood.

"No," Mole said. "There were no signs of disturbance. Yes, the doors were locked. The back one had a bolt and the bolt was shot."

"The front door?" the coroner asked.

"Sergeant Cluff opened that," the Inspector said. "It was a Yale lock."

He stood like a ramrod, his feet together, setting an example of how witnesses should behave.

"If anyone had gone out that way he could have left the door secure simply by pulling it to behind him," the coroner said.

Wright shouted, "I use my key. The lock's always on."

"Be quiet," said the coroner. "When I want to hear from you I'll let you know."

"Exactly, sir," Mole said, in a pleased, precise tone.

Mrs. Toogood, back in her seat, nudged her neighbour and nodded as if to say, "I told you so."

"But," repeated Mole, recollecting his view of the case, "there were no signs of disturbance. None at all. I looked most carefully. So did Sergeant Cluff."

"Naturally, naturally," the coroner commented dryly.

The police surgeon was jaunty, a man in a hurry, a busy man full of affairs. He had a copy of his post-mortem report, which he read rapidly.

"In other words," said the coroner, staring at the people in his court, "stripped of technical jargon, she died from gas poisoning. And you found nothing else of relevance."

The surgeon looked angry.

"Nothing," he said shortly. "Nothing."

"And the tap on the gas-pipe," the coroner said. "Stiff, we're told. Not loose."

"She was lying peacefully in bed," said the surgeon. "I saw her when I got there."

"A strong-minded woman," said the coroner, "to turn on the gas and get quietly into bed. Or a woman driven to extremity."

Wright was in the box, recalled after giving his original evidence of identification. Cluff watched him and he was nervous. He shifted his weight from foot to foot. His fingers tensed and relaxed on the rail of the box. His face was very pale. The lock of hair on his forehead was more lifeless than ever.

"Alfred Wright," said the coroner. "Twenty-eight years of age. Married for exactly thirteen months. In Gunnarshaw"—he said this distastefully, as if Gunnarshaw was the worse for it—"for almost eighteen months. Of no fixed occupation."

"Commission Agent's clerk," Wright said.

"At present?"

"Builder's labourer," Wright corrected himself.

The coroner asked silkily, "Your relations with your wife?"

"What do you mean?" Wright replied, controlling his voice with difficulty.

"What I say," said the coroner. "The difference in your ages. A little unusual, to say the least of it."

"We got on. Why shouldn't we? We had ups and downs like anyone else."

"The financial position?" said the coroner. "Who maintained the household?"

"Me."

"Exclusively?"

"As well as I could. Luck's been against me."

"Your wife had money of her own?"

"Some," Wright said, sulking. "It was her own affair."

The coroner thumbed his papers.

"Not much left, it seems," the coroner said. "Where were you on the night she died?"

"Working."

Someone tittered.

"Straight I was," Wright insisted.

The coroner settled back in his chair. He made himself comfortable. "Elaborate," he commanded.

"At Thorshall."

The coroner kept his mouth closed.

"A village seven miles away," the clerk interrupted.

"Where do you think I come from?" the coroner remarked, testily.

Wright explained. "I've been doing a job up there these last few weeks. A day or two now and again."

"Yes?" the coroner said.

"At Ghyll End."

The coroner consulted his file. "Your wife was aware of this?" he asked.

"Of course."

Mrs. Toogood whispered audibly to the woman next to her: "She said nothing to me about it."

"Did your wife object to your frequent absences?"

"I was working, wasn't I?"

"The dog. She was fond of the dog?"

"Too fond. She'd had it for years."

"And affected by its loss?"

"It might have been a kid, not a dog."

"You don't know what happened to the dog?"

"I was going to get her another."

"These spinsters," the coroner thought. "I can't imagine her as a married woman."

"I have to ask you," the coroner said. "Do you know of any reason why your wife should take her own life?"

"She wasn't well."

"Ah," said the coroner who, even after fifteen years, had a lively recollection of difficulty with his own wife in her forties. "She attended a doctor?"

"She was afraid of doctors."

"She never talked of suicide?"

"Not in so many words," Wright said slowly. "She got depressed at times."

"He's lying," Cluff thought. "She was the bravest woman I know."

They all stood up.

The coroner disappeared behind the stage. Cluff remained in the hall until the others left. He walked along a corridor to the double doors leading into the High Street. Mole was standing on the Town Hall steps, waiting for him.

"What did I tell you?" Mole said. "Suicide. While the balance of her mind was disturbed."

"It could be," Cluff thought. "If I know about loneliness, what do I know of love? She was a woman. Wright saw it and we didn't."

Inspector Mole looked up at the clock in the church-tower.

"It's hardly worth while going back to the station before dinner," Mole said. "I think I'll go home and get mine."

"When she realized her foolishness," Cluff told himself, "when she saw him as he was, after he'd married her for what he could get, a home, money—She needn't have been ashamed to admit her mistake. We'd have understood. Why hadn't we the sense to offer what Wright only pretended to offer? We abandoned her. We left her with nothing but Wright."

Mole walked away, his triumph defeated by Cluff's remoteness.

"Mr. Cluff," a voice said. "It's over, isn't it? There's nothing else the police can do?"

The reporter was a junior, his previous experience confined to weddings and funerals, the published result of his labours no more than lists of guests or mourners.

"Over?" Cluff repeated. "Over?"

"I thought for a while there was going to be some excitement in Gunnarshaw," the reporter said, in disappointed tones. "It's too much to hope for in this hole."

The High Street looked very clean, its roadway white. The sky was a hard, steely blue. The sun was brilliant, though without warmth. The air was so clear that every detail of the moors surrounding the town stood out. Light sparkled on the stained-glass windows of the church.

"There he goes," the reporter said. "They can't do anything to him. But I'd think twice about showing my face here in future if I was him."

The reporter was alone.

"Well," the reporter said aloud, "fancy Cluff going off like that, without a word."

Cluff, in Wright's wake, did not look back.

CHAPTER X

S ERGEANT CLUFF WALKED ALONG THE PAVEMENT, PAST THE shops and the banks, the library and the public houses. He did not attempt to catch Wright up. His bulk was conspicuous and, in spite of his unhurried progress, he moved with a sense of purpose. At the bottom of the street Wright turned and saw him. The Sergeant continued forward with the same deliberation.

Wright quickened his pace. He turned left, up a narrower road. He went some way along it until he came to a passageway between the buildings. He stopped there for a moment. Cluff had turned the corner too. His tweed hat was pulled well down over his eyes. One hand was in the pocket of his Burberry. He had his walking-stick in the other. Wright could hear its regular beat on the flags.

The passage along which Wright walked, not far from running now, was straight. It had high blank walls on either side. It ended at a railing, beyond which a stream flowed. The footway went off to the left, beside the railing. Cluff's footsteps echoed in the confined space of the passage.

Wright came to a bridge. The bridge was of planks laid together. On its other side wide concrete steps, with short, black strips of rubber set in them, climbed in a curve up the side of a hill. Wright reached the top of the steps. Cluff was crossing the bridge below him. Wright fled between two rows of houses.

He was going faster than ever. He forced himself not to turn his head again. He was sure he could hear that solid tread still behind him. He was hot, his forehead wet with sweat. His breath

came jerkily and his legs hardly held him up. The street he was
following brought him into Sevastopol Road.

Wright's resolution collapsed. He swung round. Cluff was
advancing at exactly the same pace, presenting exactly the same
appearance. There was no one else to be seen, not so much as a
dog moving. The house doors were closed, the neatly curtained
windows empty.

Sevastopol Road was long and surprisingly wide. It was little
used by traffic and few people in this part of Gunnarshaw owned
cars. Wright passed a grey-stone school set in a square of tar macadam. A long way ahead of him the many-windowed, soaring wall
of a mill seemed to block the street with an impassable barrier.

He strained his ears by the school, hoping to catch at least a
faint hum from its scholars. He pulled back his left sleeve to look
at his watch. The time wanted a few minutes of midday. In spite
of his isolation he did not dare to wait for the school to erupt
its children, or for men and women to crowd from the mill. He
wanted to delay until Sevastopol Road was filled with people and,
if he did, Cluff would overtake him. Balaclava Street was farther
off than ever he had known it to be.

Wright came to where the back street between Balaclava Street
and the street adjoining branched from Sevastopol Road. Though
the wider streets on to which the fronts of the houses faced were
unpaved the back streets were surfaced with square stones. These
stones were uneven. They inclined inwards from the walls of the
backyards, to a central trough. Wright stumbled and tripped up
the slope. He could see open doors over the walls, women moving
in sculleries and living-rooms. His confidence began to return.
He dodged under a line of washing. He glanced back down the

slope. Cluff was passing across the entrance to the back street. The Sergeant vanished.

Wright turned into the yard of her house, his now. He opened the back door which the police had had repaired. The window Cluff had broken had been replaced but the house was cold. He debated whether to make a fire and he was reluctant to expend the effort.

He stood in the living-room, regretting the memory he had of it when he came downstairs in the mornings. He remembered it warm, the kettle boiling on the hob, his food ready for him on the table. He was sleepy, not having slept well for the past week. It was not the fact that she had died in the bed in the room above that worried him but his recollection of her in the bed alive.

The smallness of Gunnarshaw, the knowledge of its people about each other, oppressed him. He felt suddenly that there was nowhere in Gunnarshaw he could turn, that Sergeant Cluff, if he was not around the first corner, must always be waiting round the second. They could not avoid each other. He could not get out of Cluff's way, nor the way of anyone else in Gunnarshaw. He despised its people and he knew he was cleverer than they were. He had looked on them as pigeons ready to be plucked and, when he thought about it afterwards, he had always been astonished that his projects never quite seemed to reach fruition. The people made him uneasy. His only success, his marriage, was going sour in his mouth. He had no reason to be afraid, but he felt the stab of fear.

She was up there, in the front bedroom, released by the coroner after the post-mortem. He longed for the lights and the compan-ionship of the pubs in which he had spent his evenings during the period of his marriage. He knew that even his drinking cronies would shun him if he dared to appear in public before the funeral. He was free from her importunities, her constant desire to talk to him, to hear him reply, but the house was hateful to him. The lack of her care and servile attention was worse than the urgency of her want and her loneliness.

He found himself climbing the stairs. He stopped halfway, his hand on the banister. He asked himself how it had been a bad year. He consoled himself that he knew his capacity at last. He had advanced step by step from the immaturity that had weighed on him. His wife had been the first step, and the biggest. He was no longer afraid of rebuffs. His way was clear before him.

He was in the front bedroom, the cold forgotten. He gazed at the closed coffin.

"Shall we open it for you?" they'd asked when they brought it. "It's all right. She looks the same as she always did. Perhaps people will want to see her for the last time."

"No," he'd said. "No."

Lowering his voice he'd added an apology. "I want to remember her living. Don't open it. Please."

His voice had broken artistically and, if they didn't respect him, at least they'd gone away feeling a little pity.

"Yes," he thought. "I picked you out, Amy, the first moment I saw you. I could tell what you were, from your manner, from your clothes. I could read your yearning in your eyes. You had to be the one. There was no one else with anything to give to me. All the others, they looked at me and they knew me. But your eyes were blind. You weren't stingy with your money. You imagined money could buy what you wanted. You'd more money than I dared to hope."

Wright's hand crept automatically over the inside pocket of his jacket. It caressed the bulge of his wallet.

Wright said aloud, "Surely you didn't expect me to give up everything in return for the little you had to offer me?"

Something was wrong with the room. It wasn't as it ought to be. He considered for a long time what it was before the solution came to him. He crossed the floor to draw the curtains.

Strips of thicker cloth hung down in folds on both sides of the window. A length of net shielded its lower half, concealing from people passing outside what was inside but allowing to the occupants of the room a view of the street beneath.

Wright's hand crushed the cloth of the long curtain. His heart raced, hammering in his chest for outlet. He was nailed to the boards on which he stood. If she had been rising from her coffin behind him he could not have turned to face her.

A gas-lamp was planted immediately opposite to the window, on the far pavement. At this hour only the minute flame of its pilot light showed. It was not very tall, painted green, thicker at the base, narrowing into a fluted shaft, blossoming into a lantern above an iron arm on which maintenance men propped their ladders.

Cluff leaned against the lamp, idle, nonchalant, large in the grey afternoon. His eyes were on the window through which Wright was peering. He was motionless, his face shadowed by the flopping brim of his hat, his hands in his pockets, his stick dangling from his right wrist. He stared at the net across the window as if he could see through it. The stone of the wall was no bar to his vision.

Cluff did not stir. Nor did Wright. Wright gripped the curtain, his arm raised, frozen in the beginning of motion. The afternoon began to fade. The pilot light above the time-clock in the lamp shone more brightly as the dusk gathered. If anyone in the other houses about was watching Cluff he stayed unperturbed. If it was cold where he was he gave no sign of it. No one went up the street or down it. The ordinary inhabitants of Balaclava Street never used their front doors, except for visitors. There were no visitors to Balaclava Street on a weekday.

When the lamp lit up Wright imagined he could hear the click of the mechanism releasing the flow of gas to the mantle. The light flowed into the bedroom. He was suddenly certain that Cluff would see him, darkly outlined against the window. He realized that he was shivering. The muscles of his lifted arm ached with cramp. His fingers would hardly open. He had to force himself to let the curtain go. He exercised an infinite care so that the curtain should not quiver and reveal his presence to the watcher across the street.

Wright sidled round the room against the wall. He had to cross the room, in front of the window, to reach the door on to the landing. He dropped to his knees and crawled past the coffin, pressing himself to the floor to keep below the level of the window-sill.

He fled, into the bedroom at the back, into the room where he had slept with Amy, away from Cluff. He flung himself on to the bed. Tears started into his eyes. He trembled so much that the bed creaked with his shaking. At last he pulled himself up. He sat on the edge of the bed. He dragged the quilt and the blankets free, wrapping them round him like shawls. He did not get any warmer. The darkness closed round him. There was no lamp near in the back street on to which this room faced and the blinds were drawn in the windows of the houses across from this one.

Wright could not stay where he was. He could not rest. He could not prevent himself from creeping frequently into the bedroom at the front. Always when he lifted his head carefully to the level of the window he saw Cluff still watching. There was no change in Cluff's position. For all the change there was in Cluff he might have been dead on his feet.

Wright's belly rumbled with hunger. His limbs were lumps of ice.

"What can he get me for?" Wright asked himself frantically. "There's nothing he can do. What am I frightened of?"

He started downstairs. He was determined to march along the passage. His mind was made up to throw open the front door. He was going out to face Cluff. He intended to shout, so that everyone could hear, "Hi, Cluff! What are you hanging about out there for? If there's anything you want, let me know. Get it over with, and get gone."

Wright told himself, "This is what I'll say. I'll say, 'If you don't stop spying on me I'll go to the station. I'll complain to the Superintendent. I haven't forgotten the other night. You were going to hit me then, weren't you? It was only that other constable coming in stopped you. You can't get away with this sort of thing. You don't seem to realize—we're more than halfway through the twentieth century. The police can't do as they like. Haven't there been inquiries enough? Oh no, I might not be much. But let me tell you, fellows like me aren't to be trodden on these days. Come on. If you've got anything to say, spit it out.'"

He had his hand on the handle of the door. He didn't turn the handle. He didn't go out to face Cluff. He began to try to occupy himself about the house. He made a fire in the living-room. He boiled a kettle of water. He brewed some tea and drank it.

He kept going upstairs. The window in the front bedroom was a magnet to him. He wandered up and down the passage to the front door. He edged into the downstairs parlour and out again.

Six o'clock and Cluff was still there. Seven o'clock. Eight o'clock.

"Damn him! Damn him! Damn him!" Wright sobbed.

He threw caution to the winds. A wildness seized him, a carelessness as to the consequences. He ran round the house like a madman. He switched on the lights in the passage, on the stairs, in the bedrooms. He stood by the coffin, his hand on it, upright, facing directly to the window.

He shouted, "We're up here, both of us. Are you satisfied? Can you see us now?"

He waved his other hand up and down. He ran to the window and started to push and tug at the lower frame. It was stuck and he couldn't move it. He panted as he struggled and banged his fists against the frame to jerk it loose. It moved a little and then the sashcord to his right came off its pulley, broken, snaking down on his arm.

Wright stopped fighting the window. The strength and the madness left him. He looked out in despair. Cluff stood in the middle of the street. His shoes were hidden in the grass. Wright could see the marks of his feet in a line behind him to the lamp-post.

Cluff stared up at the window. The light from the gas-lamp flickered over his shoulder. The light from the bedroom passed above his head. His face was in shadow.

Cluff turned slowly. He set off down the hill, still on the grass and mud, disdaining to walk on the flags by the houses. He stopped twice. He looked back, up at the window, as if he wanted to leave no doubts in Wright's mind.

He had gone.

CHAPTER XI

S UPERINTENDENT PATTERSON OF THE CRIMINAL INVESTIGATION
Department reached into his dip at County Police Headquarters
and took out another file. He wished fervently that he was less
concerned with administration and more directly with crime. He
read the title of the file, raising his brows a little. He opened it and
skimmed through the topmost enclosure. A minute in its margin
informed him: "The leave requested is due. There would appear
to be no objection." A question mark followed the last word.

The telephone rang. Patterson picked up the receiver. He listened and said, "Put him through."

Patterson asked, "Is that you, Cluff?"

"I wrote a letter," the telephone said.

"I have it in front of me now," the Superintendent replied.

Patterson looked out of his window. The fine weather had
vanished during the night. The window was mottled with drops
of water, dissolving here and there into tiny rivulets. The buildings he could see were black and dirty with the smoke of the city.
Their roofs were very close to the sky.

"Why?—" Patterson began. "Good God, man! At this time of
year?"

Patterson thought, "Steady, but not clever. A plodder. Where
else could I post him when he came back from the war? If he was
born in the Gunnarshaw division, he's honest. Too honest. He
thinks with his heart. There's no serious crime there. He knows the
people. He can't help finding out what he wants to find out. With
a war record like his I couldn't put him under a younger man."

"Call it urgent private affairs, if you like," came Cluff's voice.

"There's nothing wrong?" the Superintendent asked. "Nothing I can do?"

"No."

"I can't send you a relief," Patterson said. "I haven't a man available."

"I shall be at home. They could reach me there."

"What?" exclaimed the Superintendent. "At home!"

"I shan't be leaving the division. Not so far as I know."

The Superintendent shuffled papers in his file-dip:

"Wait a moment. That woman. There was a preliminary report here somewhere."

"Suicide," said Cluff. "They held the inquest yesterday."

"Of course," Patterson answered.

Cluff sounded truculent, "I'm entitled to leave. It's a long time since I had any."

"You didn't ask," the Superintendent pointed out. "When do you want to start?"

"Now."

"Unorthodox," thought the Superintendent. "He's the same age as me. He ought to have got farther than he has done. No sense of discipline. He does as he wants, but I like him. I'm not the Chief Constable."

"You know your business better than I do," Patterson said. "Fifteen days?"

"Or less," he heard Cluff say.

"Very well."

"Excuse me," Cluff said. "I'm on my way to a funeral."

"A relative?"

"Not even by marriage."

"Enjoy yourself," the Superintendent was going to say, referring to Cluff's leave. He realized the ineptness of his remark after the Sergeant's latest comment. The line went dead.

Cluff turned away from the phone.

"Annie," Cluff shouted. "I'm off."

He bent and lifted Jenet. Jenet twisted and writhed. He couldn't hold her. She jumped out of his arms and walked, dignified, to her place by the fire.

"No, Clive," Cluff said. "Not this time."

He drove away. Annie stood in the porch, shaking her head, Clive beside her, his tail drooping.

Cluff brought his car to a halt in Sevastopol Road, just past the entrance to Balaclava Street. He looked at his watch, sitting behind the wheel. After a while a hearse went by, followed by a single taxi. Both reversed up the slope and stopped near the gas-lamp by which Cluff had stood for so long after the inquest.

Cluff got out of his car. He waited at the corner, keeping well back so that he shouldn't easily be noticeable from Wright's house. A boy on a bicycle, only one hand on the handlebars, the other holding a large spray of flowers, pedalled fast from the centre of the town. He dismounted at the bottom of Balaclava Street. Cluff stepped forward, from the doorway of the grocer's shop.

"Give them to the driver," Cluff told the boy. "Ask him to put them on the coffin."

"O.K., Sergeant," the boy said.

"Look sharp," Cluff ordered. "You're late. Let me have that bicycle. I'll put it against the wall for you."

The boy examined the flowers.

"I'm sure I haven't dropped it," the boy said, pushing his cap farther on to the back of his head. "It's just as they gave it to me in the shop."

"Hurry!"

"Didn't you put a card on it, Sergeant? How will they know who it's from?"

"Don't ask questions, my lad. Just do as you're told."

The boy went up the street. The drivers of both the hearse and the taxi had gone into number thirty-three. The boy peered intently through the open front door.

The coffin came out, carried by the two drivers and by a couple of youths supplied by the undertaker. The undertaker, in a top hat and a black frock coat, looking overdressed, preceded it. Wright, by himself, followed.

They put the coffin in the hearse. The boy from the flower-shop handed his flowers to the driver.

The driver reached up to put the flowers on the coffin. Wright went to speak to him. They both searched amongst the blooms, trying to find out who had sent them. In the end Wright nodded. The driver put the spray with two wreaths on the coffin top. He closed the hearse. The undertaker got in beside the driver. Wright sat by himself in the back of the taxi and the two undertaker's men sat in the front. Hearse and taxi began to come slowly down the hill, between windows every one of which was darkened by lowered blinds or drawn curtains.

Cluff started his car. He fell in behind the taxi. They were almost at the cemetery before Wright became aware of him. The back of Wright's head in the rear window of the taxi was replaced by Wright's sharp-featured, white face. Wright's eyes opened wide.

He stared at Cluff, his expression both of surprise and fear. Cluff stared back, grimly.

There was no church service. The parson looked uncomfortable, a man not sure whether he was doing right or wrong, at odds with his conscience. He met them at the cemetery gate. His vestments clung to him damply and his bald head was wet. Part of his unease was due to his conviction that he would undoubtedly catch a cold. He regretted the nature of his office, which prevented him from wrapping up against the rain.

If the cortège from the house had been meagre quite a number of people lined the cemetery drive. The parson walked ahead of the coffin. Wright, in his place at its rear, was stalked immediately by Cluff, who had abandoned any attempt to conceal himself.

Mrs. Toogood, detaching herself from the spectators, caught up with Cluff.

Mrs. Toogood whispered, "You'd have thought he'd have asked me to go to the house. Especially when she'd no near relatives. If he wanted to put her away quietly, it didn't work out, did it?"

"I'm surprised there are so many," Cluff said. "I'm glad they came."

"She was Gunnarshaw born and bred," Mrs. Toogood told him. "We'd known her all our lives. We wouldn't let her go as he wanted. It wasn't her fault."

The parson looked back, frowning at the murmur of voices. The procession wound on its way in silence, between headstones of white marble and black marble and grey granite. The sodden grass between the graves was dark and lifeless, with no touch of fresh green about it. The flower-beds bordering the drive were empty, bereft of colour. The trees and the shrubs, which had been planted to relieve the monotony of the cemetery, were all evergreens, dull-leafed.

They got to the wall at the far end of the cemetery. Across the wall a field stretched to a river. At their feet a narrow, deep trench gashed the ground, the earth that had filled it thrown in heaps on its edges. It was crossed at either end by a stout plank on which a broad, cloth sling rested.

The graves in this part of the cemetery had no markers. They were distinguished only by the mounds remaining after they had been closed.

The people stood in a circle round the trench. The parson opened a prayer-book and began to read. Cluff stood close to Wright. He was dimly aware that women were weeping, with handkerchiefs to their eyes, or attempting to restrain their tears.

The parson gabbled, hurrying. Cluff did not listen. He willed Wright not to forget him. Wright shuffled, not watching the grave, but peering about him like a man in the grip of a waking nightmare. Sometimes he half-turned his head as if he would look Cluff in the face, but he never completed the motion. He did not know where to look. His wife's coffin was in front of him, Cluff behind him. Respect for the dead did not hide the hostility of the mourners on either side.

It was soon over. The parson hastened away to a little chapel, to change and rub his head dry on the towel his wife had made him bring. No one spoke to Wright. Wright walked rapidly along the drive, back to his taxi at the gate. He went so quickly he got there before the driver, who had found someone to talk to.

The dead woman's acquaintances walked past the taxi. Instead of looking in at Wright, they averted their heads with exaggerated care. He could not hear, as he huddled on the leather seat, in a corner, what they were saying. They were talking animatedly to each other, making up for the silence imposed on them. He knew that they were talking about him. He told himself his ordeal wouldn't last long. They couldn't assault him, or harm him. Where was the hurt in words? It was harder than he had expected to retain his calm. The future he had planned failed to give him consolation in his present situation. They could scarcely have treated him worse if they had found him standing over her with a knife in his hand, if they had caught him in the act of killing her.

He looked out of the back window. Cluff's car was there, drawn up by the roadside behind the taxi. He could see Cluff, bolt upright behind the wheel, his head touching the car hood, big and wide and capable. By Cluff's side Mrs. Toogood was not so tall, but just as disapproving. They were not talking. They had their eyes glued to the taxi. Wright could not decide which of the two he hated most.

The taxi moved off. Cluff's car crept after it. The taxi accelerated. So did Cluff.

"He's only taking her home," Wright thought. "There's nothing else he could do."

His driver heard Wright moan and wondered if he was ill.

Wright was angry with himself for not inviting Mrs. Toogood to the funeral, because he had not separated her from Cluff. He could not forget Cluff in the street yesterday. He could not forget Cluff following him home from the Town Hall. He wanted to make sure about Cluff.

He was sure already, but he still hoped.

CHAPTER XII

WRIGHT HID BEHIND THE PARLOUR WINDOW. HE PEEPED out from the side of the curtain. Cluff's car was parked by the door of number thirty-one.

Wright went back into the living-room. He strained his ears to the wall dividing his house from Mrs. Toogood's. He despaired of hearing them plainly, but he was avid to catch at least the murmur of their voices.

What were they doing in there? What were they planning?

He remembered Mrs. Toogood's hostility towards him ever since he had come to live here, her friendship for Amy.

"What do you bother with the old bitch for?" Wright had asked his wife. "You haven't been round there again, have you? She's not been in, has she?"

"But I've known her ever since I was a child," Amy said. "She's always lived next door. She knew my mother."

"Do you think I don't know? She's trying to turn you against me."

"People used to come here now and then," his wife said sadly. "Now no one comes. Don't you want me to have any friends?"

"You've got me."

"Even in the streets people don't stop and talk to me as they did."

"You're well rid of them. Can't you manage without them? Don't I mean anything to you?"

"Everything. Everything. You have to mean everything."

"If I catch you in her house—"

"I can't ignore—"

"Remember," he'd said each time he went out. "Keep away from her. Keep away from her, I tell you."

Wright listened. He could hear nothing.

"What does that woman suspect?" he asked himself. "What did Amy tell her about me?"

"She was loyal," Wright convinced himself. And this was what he had been relying on. "She wouldn't give me away. If I made sure she knew where I went, what I did, she couldn't face the shame of others knowing."

Doubt nagged at his brain.

"Who's to say it's true?" Wright asked himself. "Amy had nothing to show. I never marked her. I was careful about that."

Wright got up from the wall. He stood in front of the fire.

"Don't worry," he told his image in the mirror over the mantel. "There's nothing anyone can touch you for. It's over and done with."

He went into the parlour again. He knew without looking that Cluff's car had not gone.

"I could leave now," Wright thought. "I'm safe enough. Why shouldn't I go? Wouldn't it be as natural as staying here by myself? Did I promise, or didn't I, that I'd go back as soon as I could after the funeral?"

He argued with himself:

"No. Wait. Not until Cluff's gone."

There was a fanlight above the front door. Wright wanted Cluff to know where he was. He switched on the passage light, as he had done the night before. To make quite certain he put on the parlour light as well and drew back the curtains. He felt more secure if others, besides Cluff, saw the lights. He felt more protected from Cluff.

Wright brooded about Cluff.

"I've never done anything to him," he thought. "I haven't even been in trouble with the police in Gunnarshaw. Amy never mentioned him."

He remembered the flowers that had arrived before the funeral, unheralded, anonymous. He'd been going to ask, "Boy. Who sent these?" But the boy had gone off too quickly.

"Don't put them in. Throw them in the street," he'd been going to say to the hearse-driver. "It's just an insult."

He hadn't had the courage. He'd been afraid of the driver replying, "She's got few enough flowers. Whoever it was, it was a kind thought."

Had his wife been cleverer than he'd believed? Who else was there besides Mrs. Toogood? Mrs. Toogood had sent a wreath. Mrs. Toogood wasn't responsible for the flowers. It occurred to him for the first time that, while he had been away from his wife, his wife had been away from him. He tried to laugh away his suspicions.

"An old maid," he assured himself. "She wouldn't dare. She wouldn't know how to go about it. Who'd play fast and loose with her? Who'd want to? Good God, don't I know what she was?

"You're a fool," Wright told himself. "There wasn't a single man in forty-five years until you came along."

What was Cluff doing, aided and encouraged by Mrs. Toogood? Would Cluff spend hours watching him for nothing? Why did a policeman attend the funeral? A Gunnarshaw man, or near enough, as his wife had been a Gunnarshaw woman.

"It's impossible," Wright said loudly. "Impossible! If there'd been anything between them I'd have heard about it. I've listened to them in the pubs talking about Cluff. They wouldn't have kept quiet about a thing like that."

A metal door slammed. Wright jumped. He rushed to the parlour window. An engine sprang into life.

Cluff's car drove in a half-circle to the opposite pavement, stopped, backed, tried to go forward again. The rear wheels did not bite. They revolved uselessly. Wright was afraid the car was going to get stuck in Balaclava Street. He considered leaving his house to give Cluff a helping hand, anything so long as Cluff went away.

The tyres gripped. The car slid towards Sevastopol Road, bumping and rattling. Wright prayed that it wouldn't fall to pieces.

CHAPTER XIII

WRIGHT FELT LIGHT-HEARTED, CHEERFUL.
He switched on the radio and remembered Mrs. Toogood, and switched it off again.

He thought, "What the hell! I'll give her something to talk about."

He not only set the radio going a second time, he turned up the volume control as far as it would go.

"Tell Cluff that," he shouted at the wall. "I don't care a damn. I'm all right now. I'm in clover. You rotten old hag, you'll wish you had my luck before I've done. You'll see. You'll see!"

"Why doesn't he work?" Mrs. Toogood had said. "Why doesn't he go out and get a proper job? Is she keeping him?"

Wright made a rude gesture at the wall. "That's what I think of you," he yelled. "You interfering old busybody!"

He kept the wireless on. At intervals he looked into the street through the parlour window. He got bolder than that. He opened the front door and stepped outside to satisfy himself that the street was empty. He couldn't believe it at first. He didn't trust in the evidence of his own eyes. It was true, all the same. Cluff had given up.

He shut the door for the last time. He clicked the button on the lock. He looked at his watch and made up his mind:

"I'll go back tomorrow. First thing in the morning. I won't pass another night in this house after this one."

"Wait a minute," he thought. "Is there a will, or isn't there? 'If anything happens to me,' she said, soon after we were married, 'I want you to have everything.' 'Don't talk about it,' I said. 'What could happen to you?' I don't need a will. I get everything anyway. Twelve hundred, fifteen hundred, for the house. A hundred or two more for the furniture. What she had left in the bank."

He decided to go to bed. He went upstairs. He took off his jacket and flung it carelessly over the back of the chair by the bed. He sat on the side of the bed. His suitcase lay open on the floor. He had not troubled to unpack it properly since his return from Thorshall.

The minutes ticked away. He could hear nothing. His dreams dazzled him, alternating with his fears. His bowels were loose. He set off for the lavatory in the backyard.

Two steps led down from the threshold of the back door. Wright walked forward, searching the night in case there was someone moving in the back street. His foot sank into a soft object, but solid enough to trip him.

A nauseating stench penetrated his nostrils. He lost his balance and went flying on to the flags, landing on his hands, barking his knees. He looked at the steps in the light shining through the door. A viscous patch shone wetly. A slimy trail pointed to the sack over which he had stumbled, fetching it with him into the yard.

He rose slowly. He gazed fixedly at the sack. A sack like any other sack. A sack like the sack he'd picked up himself, more than a week ago, in the fruiterer's warehouse opposite the commission agent's.

He pulled himself together with an effort. He forgot why he was in the yard. He banged the door to behind him. He ran through the living-room, up the stairs. He seized his jacket and struggled with it to get it right way up. He grabbed his hat and his raincoat in the passage.

In Balaclava Street, in Sevastopol Road, he didn't care whether anyone saw him or not. He ran, out of Sevastopol Road, down the steps, over the stream. At the turn into the High Street he could go no farther. He could not breathe. He could not endure the pain in his side.

He crouched in a doorway, gulping, sick. He pressed his hands to his ribs. His head hung and his legs were jelly. He leaned his face against the cool glass of a window. He couldn't think straight. The dog. The dog that loved her. The dog that hated him. The dog that let the whole of Balaclava Street know every time he stepped into the house. The dog that yapped and whined. The dog, a week in the water, that had come home, sack and all.

Heavy footsteps clumped on the pavement. On the other side of the road a constable passed, stopping as he did so to try the doors of the shops. Wright shrank into his hiding-place, terrified. He waited until the steps receded, and then they were coming back. He had to move.

He edged from the doorway. He kept in the shadows of the walls and windows, grateful that it was nearly midnight.

He moved in a dead world, in a world of the dead. The night was alive but its life was inhuman, invisible. The timelessness about him, the ancient buildings between their modern counterparts, the dark church, crushed him. There was nothing in the night and the things of the night pursued him.

He was past the church, running again, driven from the shelter of the town. The rows of houses became houses semi-detached and detached. The houses ceased. The street-lamps ended by the last of them.

The night was dark, rain-clouded. The limestone walls hemming him in were ghostly. No traffic of any kind either met him or overtook him.

He was harried along the never-ending road. The country about him was immense, threatening. He could feel the chill repugnance it had for him and his own being grew smaller and smaller, until he was less than nothing. The moors towered on this side and on that. Their blackness merged with the blackness of the sky. They reached above him, groping towards each other.

Sometimes the road wound through clumps of trees, wind-bent, clinging grimly to thin soil. Under the trees the darkness was darker, the silence more perceptible, the sense of the unseen more urgent. Wright limped. His feet were pinched in his pointed, pressed-paper shoes. Blisters swelled on the tops of his toes, on his soles, under his heels. Sweat ran down his cheeks. He looked about for indications that he was coming to the end of his torment. He did not know whether he was on the right road. In spite of all his effort he seemed to make no progress.

At last he came to a sleeping village, an eternity away from Gunnarshaw. He crept through it. He had to stop more and more often. He had to lean on the walls, exhausted, drained of strength. He peered into the night, along the road by which he had come. He listened. He was sure that Cluff was coming after him.

Cluff compelled him to go on.

Another village, as silent as the last, but larger. Lines of cottages. The moors higher, heavier, wilder. Suddenly he increased his speed, regardless of the unlit windows. He hobbled and weaved, weeping at the sharp burning in his legs.

He was through the village, in an unpaved lane, climbing. Water from the moor poured down the lane. He splashed along as if he was wading in a stream, his shoes disintegrating, his trousers soaked to the knees. The mud spattered him as he pushed himself forward. He bit at the icy air, which hurt his throat and made his lungs congeal.

There was a gate in the wall to his left. Beyond the gate the lane became a track, losing itself on the open moor. Wright collapsed on to the gate. He hung there for a long time before his strength returned sufficiently for him to open it.

He crossed a yard, as muddy as the lane, between a heap of manure and doors through which came the rattling of chains and the movement of animals. A high, solid wall held back the hillside. A shed was built against it, unenclosed, housing an old Land-rover. Past the shed an opening in the wall gave on to a long flight of steps, their treads worn.

Wright crawled up the steps. He emerged on to a higher level, where a space had been flattened in the side of the hill. A barn reared over the shippons in the yard through which he had come. In front of him lay a squat, rectangular house. The trees on the slope behind it seemed to be growing out of its roof.

He dragged himself between two patches of lawn supported by the retaining wall. A carriage-way circled the wall at the foot of the steps and came back in front of the house. He crossed the carriage-way and pulled himself on to a raised, flagged walk.

A wooden porch protected the oak door of the farm. Wright fell into the porch. After a while he began to hammer the door with his fists. His blows were weak, little thuds on the wood. He waited.

No one answered.

Wright beat again on the door panels.

Nothing moved in the house.

He struck and struck in frenzy.

CHAPTER XIV

"**M**OTHER!"

The girl was young, no more than seventeen. She was rosy with sleep. Her body was firm and well-shaped. She wore a nightdress that was almost transparent. The nipples of her breasts were sharp and stiff and pointed. Her belly was flat, her thighs rounded. Her brown, wavy hair was muzzed about her face.

The girl slept in a bedroom at the front of the house. The room was scented with youth, warm with the dreams of the night. The bed was hollowed where she had been lying. The pillow she had clasped to herself in her loneliness was crushed with the vision of her hopes.

"Mother!" the girl called again.

She stood, looking out into the street from the window of number thirty-four, not yet quite ready to face the day.

Her mother shouted, "You'll be late. Hurry up! Hurry up!"

"But he's there," the girl objected to herself. "Just as he was for so long the night before last."

She remembered him by the lamp, watching and waiting, strong and virile. He was old, and what was callow youth to her? What had she to do with acned, inexperienced boys, wanting to lead her on Saturday nights into the dark ginnels off the High Street, wanting to press their amateur kisses on her lips, with a grating of teeth, in the fields in summer?

"What are you looking at, Jean?" her mother asked.

Her mother was grey and bent, untidy in her working-clothes, with no figure left.

Jean looked at her mother and thought, "I'll never let myself get like that. I won't live all my life in a house in a street. I won't nag and whine as if there wasn't such a thing as love in the world. I'll always be neat and attractive. My love will last. My husband won't be driven to distraction, a piece of furniture like anything else in the house, worn and useful, but not a man any more, not a man as a man ought to be."

"You'll be late," her mother repeated. "And you'll catch your death of cold in that disgusting thing. They'll see you from the street."

Her mother was by her side at the window.

"He's not satisfied," her mother said. "He's right not to be satisfied. The coroner's a fool."

"I've seen him often in the town," Jean said, innocently. "A policeman, isn't he—a detective?"

"Don't you know Cluff yet?" her mother replied. "Where have you been all your life?"

"He's not married," Jean said, knowing much about him.

"Not him," her mother told her. "An old bachelor. He's not the marrying kind."

Cluff had crossed the street. He turned the handle on the door of number thirty-three. He knocked, but he couldn't get in. He looked at the windows on the upper storey. Jean imagined that he sighed. His head moved and she was certain that he saw her. Her heart leapt. Cluff passed up the slope of Balaclava Street.

"What will Mr. Greensleeve say if you're not there by nine?" Jean's mother said. "Your breakfast'll be cold too."

A cindered footpath separated the end of the row of houses from a pasture where sheep grazed. Cluff rounded the gable of the last house. He walked down the back street. Women, busy about their household duties, glanced up from their tasks and wondered.

The Sergeant pushed open the gate of Amy Wright's house. He halted, with his hand on the gate. He saw the sack under the living-room window, moved from where he had left it on the doorstep. He smiled.

Cluff put his hand on the back door. It swung open at his touch.

"Wright," Cluff shouted. "Wright!"

He entered and went through the scullery into the living-room. The lights were on and he switched them off. He climbed the stairs to the bedroom she had slept in and died in. He noticed the suitcase at once.

The case was cheap, made of a substitute for leather. It held a cheap suit, a shirt and a handkerchief. A safety-razor and the remains of a bar of shaving soap were wrapped in a piece of tissue paper. The paper had stuck to the end of the soap as the soap dried.

Cluff shook out the suit. He went through each pocket in turn. He let the suit drop and stared about him. His eyes strayed slowly, fastening for long minutes on each segment of the room. They came to rest on a wallet, humped as it had fallen from a pocket. The wallet lay half-under the bed, an inverted V, between the bed and a chair by the bed.

He emptied the wallet. He found currency notes, some pencilled slips of paper, the writing rubbed and indistinct, a postage stamp or two. There was one letter, still in its envelope. The envelope was addressed to Wright in a woman's hand, care of the commission agent at the office off the High Street. Behind the envelope a snapshot showed a woman posed by a five-barred gate. The wall of a house rose beside her. Hills formed a black background to the picture.

He read the letter, his face showing his disgust at its contents. He looked for a long time at the snapshot. He thought that age meant nothing. He told himself that a woman in her thirties could be more lecherous and lustful and abandoned than a girl of seventeen, as shameless, hotter for a man, driven by the known, the experienced, her body, which had memory in it, crying out for repetition.

"It never ends," Cluff said quietly. "They go on like that to the grave. Like drunkards they stop caring what they get. Anything will do to satisfy them, anything in the shape of a man, Wright as well as any other."

Cluff crammed both letter and photograph into his pocket. His step, as he left the house, was jaunty, his expression content.

"Sergeant!" Barker exclaimed in surprise, looking up from his desk. "Aren't you on leave? There's a letter here, in this morning's mail. They spoke to you on the telephone—"

"Mole," Cluff said. "He checked on Wright's story?"

"It was your job," Barker thought. "You shouldn't have thrown in your hand like that. You shouldn't have left it to Mole. He's angry about it. He's making a report."

"Leave it alone," Barker pleaded. "It's done with now."

"Well?" Cluff asked.

"You've seen his statement," Barker said.

"Pointing a barn!" Cluff spat.

"He knew how to do it." Barker's voice had a note of pity in it. "Mole rang up Thorshall. It was true."

"Seven miles," Cluff said. "How long would it take you to walk it?"

"Two hours," Barker replied, after a pause.

"The nights are long in winter," Cluff said. "Two hours here. Two hours back."

"No," Barker objected. "No. It isn't possible. Someone would have seen him. Someone would have heard him."

Cluff said, "Her dog was missing. She didn't have her dog."

"You saw the house," Barker protested. "Would she watch him turn on the gas and listen to him go and stay in the bed to die?"

"Yes," Cluff said. "I think she would."

Barker's young face looked shocked. His eyes were wide, his lips apart. The colour in his cheeks faded. Words tumbled in his mind, unable to escape. "You," the words said, "the most normal, the most stolid, the most down-to-earth of us all. Your feet on the ground, rooted in the soil. Everything about you—what people mean when they talk of the countryman, the farmer, the man brought up amongst these hills. Unshakable. Unimaginative. Men like you don't go off the rails. They don't have ideas. Only facts mean anything to them."

"Must we always start with a struggle?" Cluff asked wearily. "With resistance? With clinging to life? Does there always need to be violence in murder?"

"It's no good," Barker stammered, trying to hold fast to a link with sanity.

"Don't you see?" Cluff thought. "I knew her. I knew what she was. I knew the mistake she'd made. I knew she had no way out. She wanted to die."

"Murder with the full co-operation of the victim," Barker was thinking. "If she was asleep?—If she didn't hear him?—She must have heard him. Anything else is too much to believe. He couldn't rely on her not waking up. Or could he? If she had woken up, would he have waited until another time? I can't believe it."

"She knew what he'd brought her to," Cluff said.

"Sergeant," Barker pleaded. "Isn't there somewhere you can go these next two weeks? The seaside perhaps. Or London. Where you'll see new faces, where you don't have to think about this."

"You're a good fellow, Barker," Cluff said. "But young. You know where to find me if I'm needed."

The Sergeant was opening the door to go out. Barker raised himself in his chair. He had his fists on the desk, supporting his body on stiff arms. He leaned forward:

"Sergeant! If I can help. In my free time. When I'm off duty—"

"It's good of you," Cluff said. "But you're not a Gunnarshaw man. It's my pigeon."

CHAPTER XV

SERGEANT CLUFF LEFT HIS CAR OUTSIDE THE BOTTOM YARD at Ghyll End. He let Clive out, warning, "Stay close. Heel! Heel!"

He looked up at the barn above the shippons, burrowing farther into the hill. He passed by the shed near the steps that led up to the level of the house and stared at the Land-rover. He climbed between the two patches of lawn, on to the drive in front of the house.

Behind the barn a line of loose-boxes, their floors higher than the barn floor, extended from the barn to join the gable end of the house. In the oblong, rising, three-sided space formed by the extension of the boxes and the barn and the end wall of the house stood a wheelbarrow, with a spade in it. There were traces of mortar on the cobbles. A ladder reared against the barn.

He lifted his hand to knock at the door. The line of the house, at the end farthest from the barn, was broken by a dairy, which jutted nearer the driveway. The door to the dairy was at right-angles to the farm's main door.

The Sergeant let his hand fall to his side. He trod softly on the stone floor of the dairy. A second door led out of it into a wash-kitchen, with a huge copper encased in brick above a firehole.

He came into a backyard. A wall opposite to him held back the hill. Geese, above the level of his head, peered over the wall. The entrance to the living-kitchen and its window were to his left. From round a corner to his right he heard the grunting of pigs. Their smell was strong.

The geese were noisy. He hadn't reckoned with them giving warning of his approach. The door of the kitchen opened before he had a chance to reach it. The woman in the snapshot confronted him, her manner hostile and suspicious.

She was older than she had seemed in the photograph, but younger than she appeared, less attractive in the clothes she was wearing than when she had posed for the camera. To look at her she did not seem capable of the adolescent sentences, scrawled in untidy, ill-formed handwriting, Cluff had read in her letter. He could not believe she knew anything of romance. She was close, on the farm, to the mechanics of reproduction, the breedings, the calvings and the lambings. His eyes roved over her shoulder, into what he could see of the kitchen. There was nothing to indicate the presence of children. Her husband was a vague recollection in his mind, which he could not recall with clarity.

Sleep congealed in minute ivory globules at the corners of her eyes. She had not washed that morning. Her wispy hair was greying. If she had ever been shapely her shape had sagged into looseness. Big warmly-lined boots, their leather stained with dry mud, covered her feet. Her thick stockings were wrinkled. Her skirt hung askew round her waist. A tattered cardigan stretched across her swollen breasts. She had small eyes, pig-like and greedy.

She barred Cluff's way. He pushed past her into the kitchen. It was cleaner than herself, but higgledy-piggledy, its atmosphere the sort she would create, inevitably, wherever she was. The table against the wall was set for two. A big fire blazed in the old-fashioned range. A kettle spouted steam on the hob.

Cluff stood with feet apart, his back to the fire. He listened intently. The woman listened too. He caught her more than once glancing swiftly at an inner door, which must lead to a staircase somewhere and to the front of the house. Her eyes shifted and she fidgeted uneasily.

"What do you want?" the woman asked.

Had he heard movement over his head, or not?

"It's not far to where I was born," he said, "over the tops."

"Cluff's Head," she replied. "You don't remember me. I knew you when I was a little girl."

"You must have been a lot younger than Cricklethwaite."

"His second wife," she said.

"Dead, I heard."

"Six months ago."

Cluff thought, "And you were free. For the first time. Your own mistress. Subordinate to no one, not to the parents of your youth, not to the husband of your middle years."

She watched him study the table.

She said, "He went right away. As soon as he read about it."

Cluff understood that she was speaking now, not of her husband, but of Wright.

"Did he sleep here?" Cluff asked.

"Why not? He worked for me as he could. It's not easy to go backwards and forwards to Gunnarshaw with the bus service as it is."

"The two of you alone in the house?"

"Think what you like."

"Where is he?"

"Can't you leave him alone?"

"Here? Upstairs?"

"Get out!" she said. "I don't want you here."

He was not mistaken. He could not be certain of the direction of the sound. Lies were implicit in her manner and in the arrangement of the table. She backed to the inner door, standing in front of it with her arms akimbo. He took a step forward and she faced him without moving.

Her eyes mocked him, bold. Her face was brazen. She laughed at him. He swung round sharply. An old man grinned at him, coming into the kitchen from the yard.

The woman drew her lips from her black teeth in a travesty of a smile. She hissed, "You don't think I can run the farm by myself?"

She said to the old man, "Your dinner's nearly ready. Too close for you to start another job."

"Caleb Cluff," the old man said.

His boots were filthy below his woollen stockings patched with darns. His corduroy knee-breeches were stiff with dirt. His threadbare tweed jacket stank of cow manure. He was an odorous old man, his odour compounded of himself and his animal charges.

The woman sidled to the oven by the fire. She looked inside.

The woman said, "Ben works for me. He lives in the village, but he has his meals here. He eats with me, when I do."

"I wondered whose car it was," Ben said. "Is he up about Wright?"

"Ask him," the woman said.

Cluff said, "Yes, I am."

"You're wasting your time," Ben told him. "We don't expect him back for a day or two. You'll allow a chap that when his wife's just gone."

Cluff said nothing.

"I'm none so good on ladders nowadays," Ben said. "The barn's pretty high."

"And old," the woman said.

"It wanted doing badly," Ben explained.

His eyes were cunning. He spoke with confidence, leering at his mistress. He put out his hand to Clive, who was sitting quietly, waiting Cluff's pleasure.

"One of your brother's breeding?" Ben asked. "He keeps good dogs at Cluff's Head."

Cluff stared pensively at the door into the rest of the house. He was disappointed rather than angry. The table had deceived him. Whatever he had heard had been from Ben, not from upstairs.

Cricklethwaite's widow watched him insolently. Ben sucked with his tongue at a hollow tooth in the back of his jaw. His smell was stronger as the heat of the fire warmed him.

Cluff put his hat on his head.

The woman said, "Not that way. Through here."

She led him into a short passage, not hiding her triumph. Stairs on his right mounted to the upper part of the house, turning back on themselves halfway. In front of him an open door revealed a pantry. It had stone shelves, at waist-level, and a small, high window looking on to the barn.

She took him into a living-room, opposite to the stairs across the passage. He had to take his time in order not to tread on her heels. He gazed about him as she intended he should do. Sides of bacon and hams, wrapped in white muslin, hung on hooks fixed in the ceiling beams. Her eyes looked up, matching his.

"That's right," she said. "That's my bedroom up there."

He crossed the raised, flagged walk. She was still by his side. She put her hand on his arm, guiding him away from the steps that descended to the lane.

"It's easier by the barn," she told him.

She swung back one leaf of the huge barn door effortlessly. He did not object. Her arms were brawny under the unravelling sleeves of her cardigan. Her muscles knotted as she pulled on the iron ring that served for a handle.

He thought, "She's too close to the earth. What she can't get in other ways she'll have by force. She won't mind pain and suffering if they're not her own. Cricklethwaite was a brute. He ruled his beasts with a stick. He'd rule her in the same fashion."

They crossed the barn. Hay was stacked on both sides of them. To their left an inner flight of steps led under the stone platform supporting the hay, to the shippon beneath where cows shifted in their stalls. A free space by the wall to the right of the door, bordered with feed bins, gave access up more steps at the back of the barn to the loose-boxes.

She took him between the two haymows to a smaller door, facing the main entrance, and out on to the steeply sloping hillside. His car was below him, by the bottom yard.

"Satisfied?" she asked. "Everybody is but you."

Cluff walked away with Clive.

She called after him, "The police don't want Wright. I read the papers. I saw the inquest report. What are you—judge or detective?"

Cluff went on his way.

"Shall I tell him," she shouted, "when he comes to finish the barn, you're looking for him?"

He did not get into his car at once. He stood in the lane. Clive stretched at his side to nose his fingers.

He filled his pipe and lit it. A cloud of smoke floated about his head. The air was still, the sky low and grey, the moors closing in. Down on the road the houses in Thorshall were solid and forbidding, not accretions on the country, but growing from it, as the people who lived in them did.

Ben leaned on the gate of the bottom yard. Drops of moisture strayed from his nose to pearl his moustache. Cluff and the old man glared at each other for a while.

"You've been quick with your dinner," Cluff said, breaking the silence.

"She sent me to see if you'd gone."

Cluff shrugged.

"I'll stay put till you do," Ben said. He looked through Cluff as if Cluff did not exist.

Time passed.

Ben said, as if to himself, "He was here when I went home that day. He was here when I came back in the morning."

"She told you to say that."

"Aye. She told me. You need telling."

Clive whimpered, nudging Cluff.

"It's not the first time I've said it," Ben continued. "Ask the policeman yonder."

He paused.

He said, "The Cluffs was always a stubborn lot. You couldn't tell 'em owt."

CHAPTER XVI

C LUFF PULLED UP BY THE "BLACK BULL" IN THE VILLAGE.
The inn door was open. He went inside with Clive. Neither
customers nor landlord were in evidence.

The bar was at the end of a passage. An oak settle stood at
right-angles to the fire. The bar counter was opposite to the
fire, against the rear wall. Round black-oak tables and spindle-
backed chairs dotted the space between bar and fire. Benches,
their seats padded with shiny, black leather, ranged the remaining walls.

The Sergeant sat on the settle, Clive at his feet. No one came
in. For all the notice that was taken of Cluff the pub might have
been his. He was cold from staying so long in the lane. He bent
over the fire, letting the heat flow into him.

A big, octagonal-shaped clock, its once-white face browned
with age, ticked above the mantel. Here and there in the dim room
horse-brasses glinted in the light cast by the flames.

"Since you've lost your voice," Cluff heard, "try this."

A hand thrust a pewter tankard under his nose.

"Couldn't you have shouted?" the landlord asked. "I was out
at the back."

"I'd have shouted when the fire went down," Cluff said.

"It's nobbut middling now," his host said.

The landlord picked up a log from a basket by the settle and
threw it on the fire. He added. "It's not often we see you this way."

"Not often enough," Cluff said.

The landlord looked at him quizzically.

"You'll not have had anything at Ghyll End," the landlord stated. "Would a slice or two of beef do, with a few onions, and bread and cheese? Maggie's at Gunnarshaw market."

"There's not much you miss," Cluff replied.

"Joe's lad saw you going up the lane. I'll have a bite with you, seeing as I'm on my own."

"Well, George," Cluff said, through a full mouth, "how's things with you?"

"So-so," George replied. "I got rid of my lambs a three-week past. Mind you, if it wasn't for the pub helping out the farm—"

"Ghyll End looked in poor shape."

"Cricklethwaite tended it all right. He knew his job."

The Sergeant said, "I've been spending too much time in Gunnarshaw. I'm out of touch."

"I didn't like the chap," George said, "but I'll say that for him."

"I'm surprised she kept the farm on."

"Aye," said George, "Ben Crier's not much help. You can't tell with females."

"It's a long time," Cluff mused. "She knew me but I had to think before I could recall her. I'm not clear about her now. I must have been in my teens and she only a little lass."

"Flighty," George commented. "Cricklethwaite drove her with a tight rein. Not like his first."

"Why he married her, maybe," Cluff said.

"He'd be fifty when he took her. She not much more than twenty."

"Hard for her," Cluff replied.

George took a forkful of meat. He chewed thoughtfully.

"They didn't get on," George said. "Perhaps she'll do better next time."

The Sergeant applied himself to his food.

George said, "You can't blame her for sampling the goods before she buys. Not when she's been caught once."

"Like that?" Cluff murmured.

"There's more goes on at Ghyll End than pointing a barn," George said.

They went on eating.

"What about Ben Crier?" Cluff asked.

"He knows when he's well off. She's got him where she wants him."

George went to the bar and pulled a couple of pints.

"You thinking of taking a farm?" George said.

"No."

"There's nothing to stop you having a look at Ghyll End if you like," said George.

He returned to the fire with the beer.

"That chap's wife died convenient," George said.

"She hasn't waited long," Cluff remarked, thinking of the woman at the farm.

George picked his teeth with his thumbnail. He leaned back in his seat and stretched out his legs to the fire. He murmured, "He went sudden in a way, did Cricklethwaite."

"He'd had his life out."

"He wasn't one for doctors," George said. "Not that ours is much use."

"Old Dr. Henry? He brought me into the world."

"He did the same for most of us."

"I've seen him out in all weathers," Cluff said. "He'd ride horse-back through the drifts if he couldn't get any other way."

"He stuck to that trap of his into the thirties," George said. "There's none about here but likes him." He paused. "But you'd not call him one for progress. He'd always get there, only what good was he when he did?"

"You die of old age in these parts. There's not much he needs to know."

"If you say so."

"Wasn't that what Cricklethwaite died of?"

"You know where the doctor lives."

"I'm asking you."

"It got to where Cricklethwaite couldn't keep his beer down, let alone his provender."

"It happens," Cluff said.

"Ulcers, according to the doctor."

"He ought to know."

"Too late when she called Henry in. But Cricklethwaite wouldn't have him. I can't say different."

It was a long time before Cluff spoke again.

"Let me use your phone, George," Cluff said.

"It's not been shifted," George replied.

"Hello," Cluff said into the telephone. "John? I'm coming up for a few days."

He listened and added:

"That's so. I'm taking a holiday."

His brother said, "It's all right, Caleb."

"I'll get some things together," Cluff said. "Expect me when you see me."

"You're welcome."

He left the telephone. Cricklethwaite's widow was standing in the passage.

She said, "That'll be nice for you."

George interrupted from the bar.

"Here," George said. "It's after closing time. I should have bolted that door before now."

"When does your holiday start?" the woman asked Cluff. "Tomorrow?"

She turned to George. "The usual," she said. "No. Make it two packets this time."

George produced the cigarettes she wanted. She paid him and went out smiling. Cluff followed her to the door. He stood there and watched her down the village street.

She could feel Cluff's eyes on her back. She knew other eyes were plotting her progress from cottage windows.

"There she goes," one wife said to another.

"It's a wonder she dare mix with decent folk," the second replied.

"A bitch," said the first. "And Cricklethwaite not half a year in his grave."

Jinny Cricklethwaite turned into the lane for Ghyll End. Her pace slackened. Her brain was busy. She walked automatically, seeing nothing.

Ben Crier was waiting in the farmyard. He said, "He's here, isn't he?"

"If you know," Jinny said, "you don't need to ask."

"I didn't bargain for this," the old man said. "Cluff won't let go."

"You! Bargain!" she exclaimed contemptuously. "It's too late for you to bargain."

"Is it?" Ben demanded. His face twisted. "With you, maybe. There's others."

She made for the house.

She stopped and called, "Come up. I've something for you."

He turned into the shippon, muttering, "That's always your answer," ignoring her.

She heard the clatter of a shovel scraping up cow droppings.

Her eyes glittered.

CHAPTER XVII

S HE TRIED TO LOSE HERSELF IN WRIGHT. HE WHINED AND
protested in her arms. He talked endlessly about Cluff.

The dark night enveloped them. She lay loose in the bed. She
could see the room about her clearly, without the aid of light.

She remembered her husband. She could hear Cricklethwaite
hawking, his breath wheezing in his chest. She could feel the rise and
fall of the mattress as he got up in the blackness to relieve himself
and came back in again. His gnarled hands played in her soft, flabby
flesh. The nausea his fumblings inspired flooded into her mouth.
The futility of his aged, worn-out body filled her with loathing.

The morning released them, but only from the bed.

Wright wandered like a spirit in purgatory. His feet rang on the
concrete of the backyard. He climbed into the croft and the geese
retreated, screeching. Frightened he fled to the wash-kitchen and
the dairy. The pigs grunted hungrily when he passed the sty. The
barn doors creaked as he pulled them open.

She watched him from the front window. He stood at the top
of the steps going down to the lane. His head moved slowly as his
eyes searched the hillsides.

He was hunched by the fire in the living-kitchen. His hairless
hands trembled over the flames. His limbs were shaken by invol-
untary spasms. He was off again, stumbling round the buildings.
Doors opened and closed. The animals, catching his unease, pulled
nervously at their ties.

She could settle to nothing herself. Anger boiled in her. Must she
always be cursed in her men? She bottled her emotion inside her,

compelling herself to silence. If he had anything to be frightened of, she had more. She was jealous, comparing it with her own, of the life Wright had had already.

They sat at the table. He hardly tasted anything. He dabbled with his fork in the contents of his plate. The anger born in her, fathered by his ineffectiveness, grew. When they needed courage he had none and she must provide courage for them both.

She was infected by his obsession with Cluff. She dwelt on Cluff more and more. What did Cluff know? Why had Cluff come to the farm? How far back did his knowledge go?

His fear of Cluff became her fear of Cluff. The country whispered to him with voices his colleagues could not hear. He could feel as well as see. He was a simple man, elemental. He was grim as the country was grim.

"Where's Ben?" Wright asked again and again.

She told him as often, "Ben's gone to the moor to gather the sheep."

"Are you sure? Are you sure?" he demanded.

He was afraid of Cluff. He was afraid of Ben. Ben said little to him in words. Ben said much with his eyes. Ben grinned at Wright and asked Jinny offhandedly, "Let me have a pound or two. My pockets are empty." She gave it to him.

Ben on the moor, but they could not get rid of Ben. Ben doing as he liked, treating the house as his own property. The farm going down, people in the village talking. Ben going off at nights to his cottage. The woman spying on him, he spying on the woman.

Wright's voice was a shout. "Why today? Why to the moor today? Did you see him go? Are you certain?"

She struggled for patience. She said, "The sheep must come down. Who would listen to Ben?"

"Cluff would listen," he insisted. "Cluff would listen to anything from anybody."

"What time did he go?" Wright wanted to know. "How far is it? Why isn't he back?"

"He can't go in an hour," she replied, swallowing the words that welled in her.

Wright gazed at the moor. It rolled away, over the skyline. It rose in peaks and screes. It dropped into hollows and bogs. Perpendicular black crags raised themselves above still black pools of peat-stained water. Jumbled rocks poked from soft, springy earth. The trenches of tiny streams crossed expanses of heather and bilberries. Conifers dotted the slopes in close-planted patches, dead trees strewn round the roots of the survivors.

On the moor Ben went slowly. He had no flock about him. No dog quartered the wilderness at his command. He did not look as if he was shepherding. His mind would not let him stop.

He lay in the heather on the crest of the moor, above the next dale. He looked down. A long way below, like a child's toy, he saw Cluff's Head. Its buildings were firm amongst rough pastures. A windbreak of trees shielded it from winter gales. Smoke rose peacefully from its chimneys. His conscience pricked. He was old, with sin on his soul.

A black speck that was a man climbed up from Cluff's Head. He had a dog with him. He came steadily up to the moor top, with a moorman's unhurried stride. He passed over the moor some distance from where Ben watched.

Ben stayed quiet. Cluff's figure dwindled. Ben got up and followed. He kept to the shelter of the crags. He hugged the hollows
beneath the horizon. He bent his body double as he crossed the
rises.

The Sergeant took the easiest tracks. His dog bounded far in
front, unrestricted. He came to where he could see Ghyll End,
where the moor separating it from Cluff's Head descended. He
looked over the slopes Ben had climbed. He watched Ghyll End
as Ben, on the other side, had watched Cluff's Head.

Ben crouched in the bracken. The Sergeant sat on a rock. Clive,
called to him, lay panting.

Ben backed. He retreated behind a spur of the moor. He went
in a wide circle, through a plantation, and plunged into the ghyll
that gave Cricklethwaite's farm its name. The ghyll was a deep
cleft in the ground, dug by a stream in a fault between hard rocks.
The stream sank farther each year into its bed. Hawthorn trees
and hollies on its steep banks shut it in as with a roof. Ben slipped
and slithered in sticky mud, clambering over rocky outcrops that
defeated the scouring of the water.

The high wall of the croft rising above the level of the kitchen
window screened off most of the late afternoon light. The room
was dark, lit only by the leaping flames of the fire. They sat quietly, wearied of talking, in a silence intensified by the ticking of a
clock, eerie in the stillness. The noises of the farm had died away
as the day was dying. Time and place and life itself were unreal
and shadowy.

Wright started. His hand went to his mouth. He stared, hypno-
tized, at the gently opening door. Jinny Cricklethwaite stiffened,
her body rigid. The clock ticked louder.

Ben leaned against the door. His head drooped on his chest. The thinness of his hair revealed his dirty scalp. His legs were unsteady. He fought for breath. His boots were plastered. Fresh mud daubed his stockings and breeches. The sleeve of his jacket was torn. His face was a death's-head in the firelight, transparent, with the texture of parchment. Saliva dribbled from the corners of his mouth.

"He's there," Ben said.

Wright uttered a sharp, brief cry. He half-rose and collapsed back into his chair. The woman stared at Ben, saying nothing. Her eyes roved over him from head to feet, taking in every detail of his appearance. She looked at the window. Finally she asked, in a low voice, sibilant:

"Did you speak to him?"

Ben hesitated and shook his head.

Wright sprang to his feet. He seized Ben and pushed him out into the yard.

"Where?" Wright screamed. "Where?"

Ben tottered through the wash-kitchen and through the dairy. He lifted an arm in the lowering dusk and pointed to the edge of the moor.

"Where? Where?" Wright was still asking, his townsman's eyes blind.

"I'll get the glasses," the woman said.

She gave the binoculars to Wright.

"This way from the far plantation," she said coldly. "Where the rocks rise against the sky."

"It's not true," Wright mumbled.

"It's true," she said and smiled.

"Come back! Come back!" the woman shouted.

Wright whirled.

She ran after Ben, who had set off for the lane. She grabbed Ben's arm. She struggled with Ben. She dragged and pulled him. Her strength was greater than his.

"Where are you off to?" she asked, in brittle tones. "Where are you going?"

Ben muttered and Wright could not make sense of his mutterings. Wright looked again at the moor, through the binoculars. He saw Cluff get to his feet. Cluff stood upright, still.

The binoculars were a part of Wright. They were rooted to his eyes. He looked and looked and looked again. He opened his mouth to speak, and closed it. Not until certainty became more than certainty could he say, "He's gone."

"He's at Cluff's Head," Ben said. "I saw him come up from there."

"The more fool him," Jinny Cricklethwaite murmured. Her voice made Wright tremble.

CHAPTER XVIII

S HE CAME INTO THE KITCHEN BEHIND THEM. SHE TURNED the key in the lock of the door.

The edge of the stone sink under the window pressed into her buttock. She was big and hard in the waning firelight.

Ben sat small in a chair across the hearth. Wright huddled on a chair by the table, opposite the fireplace, his elbows on the table, his face buried in his hands.

"You fool!" she said. "You fool!"

Wright lifted his head. He realized only slowly that she was addressing him. The depth of her hatred shattered him with the force of a physical blow. She swelled and grew monstrous.

"If you hadn't come here yesterday," she said, each word spaced from the next, her voice low. "If you'd stayed in Gunnarshaw as I told you to do."

Her eyes bored into him.

"You led him here," she added. "This is because of you."

"What else could I do?" he managed.

"It was you he wanted," she said. "Not me. You've shown him what he'd never have known. He'd forgotten I existed. Cricklethwaite was nothing to him."

"He was watching me," Wright pleaded. "I had to get away from him."

"All you had to do," she said with infinite contempt, "was to face him, to let time pass. He was powerless."

"I couldn't," he excused himself. "I couldn't."

She said with deliberation, meaning every syllable, "I could kill you."

"All this," she said, and her arm swung to take in her years at the farm. "All this to be paid for. My plans and my patience and my dreams. I won't give it all up now. Not for Cluff. Not for you. Not for anyone."

Ben moaned.

"They'll dig Cricklethwaite up," Ben said. "They'll find out. It makes no difference how long they've been buried."

The scales fell from Wright's eyes. Knowledge replaced the suspicions he had refused to admit. His voice rose high. He shrieked:

"I didn't do that. I'd no part in it."

"You knew," she mocked him.

"How did I know?" Wright complained. "When did I ask you about it?"

"Who's going to believe you?" she said.

"No," said Wright. "No. And the night my wife died. I was here. You've said so already. You can't go back on it. Would I have gone to them if I'd killed her, of my own free will?"

"I had to drive you to it," she said.

She moved from the sink. She towered broad and threatening over Ben Crier. He shrank into himself as she bent over him. Wright leaned forward, terror in his face. Her words struck at Ben like the fangs of a snake.

"Dig him up?" she said. "And find what's in him?"

"I won't tell," the old man stammered, pushing at her with weak arms.

She said, "And you knew it was there. You saw me prepare

the food I gave him. You've had what I could give. You've put your filthy hands on me."

"No," Ben cried. "No! No! No!"

"What do you want to do?" she asked. "Save your neck at the expense of mine?"

"I don't know anything," Ben begged.

"Did you tell Cluff?" she screamed. "Did you? Did you?"

"As I hope for salvation," the old man sobbed.

Her fingers clawed Ben's shoulders.

She said quietly, "Just now. You were off to the village. To the police. To say, 'She murdered her husband. I'm an old man. She made me hush it up. I have to tell.'"

"I won't tell. I won't tell," Ben groaned.

"An old man," she said. "Life's sweet to you, the sweeter because you've so little left. The old are selfish."

Her eyes were slits, her face contorted.

"Life's sweeter to me," she went on. "And I'm selfish too. So I'll let you go, with Cluff here today and yesterday, and Cluff coming back tomorrow?"

She glanced from Ben to Wright.

"Two of you," she said. "It's one too many. I can't watch you both."

"Jinny! Jinny!" Wright said, desperately.

She scooped up the cloth of Ben's jacket. She shook Ben like a terrier does a rat.

"Did Cluff see you coming down the moor?" she demanded. "Did he? Did he?"

Ben's head wobbled. His few teeth jarred together. His eyes closed. She could hardly hear him when he stammered, "He didn't see me. I came down the ghyll."

"Jinny," Wright said again.

"Wait," she told Wright. "Keep him there in the chair. Watch him!"

She flung back at Wright from the door to the front of the house, "You can't get away. Whatever you do I'll swear you killed your wife. I'll make them believe it."

She was back.

She had a double-barrelled shotgun cradled in her arms. The old man and the young man stared at her, deprived of action.

Ben's jaw dropped. His mouth fell open.

Her lips parted. "It's all right," she said. "I'm not going to shoot you, Ben."

She raised the gun by the barrels and brought the stock down on Ben's head. He made no effort to avoid it. The sound of the blow was loud in the kitchen.

Ben collapsed sideways in his chair. His trunk folded over the chair arm. His right hand dangled, touching the floor. The fingers twitched.

She turned to Wright.

"There," she said, propping the gun against the wall. "You'd no part in what happened to my husband. You were here the night your wife died. But you've a part in this. Deny it if you can."

She pulled at Ben's lapel, overturning him on to the floor. She picked up the cushion on which Ben had been sitting. She advanced with it on Wright, bearing him back against the sink until the sink stopped him from going farther.

"Take it," she commanded.

She thrust the cushion into Wright's hands.

He felt the pain of her grip. He heard her say, "Over his face."

She was breaking him in two. She was forcing him down, on to his knees. Her hands crept along his arms. Her soft body pressed into his back. His hands were in hers. The cushion came lower, over Ben's mouth and nostrils. Her weight knocked him flat on top of the cushion. He was buried beneath her and Ben was buried beneath him.

She was panting. Wright was panting. The fire was very low. They were black and shapeless, entangled in the near dark. Their slightest movement was exaggerated and gigantic on the wall.

She heaved herself to her feet. She hauled Wright after her. The cushion slipped from Ben's face. His eyes accused them.

She threw Wright away. He stumbled and snatched at the table. Her breasts rose and fell as she drank in gulps of air. She fought for self-control.

"Get the horse harnessed," she ordered. "Put the chains on him."

She stepped closer. He was afraid that she was going to strike him. He staggered through the living-room and out of the front door. She ran after him with a lantern.

"In the sledge," she said. "You know where it is."

The lantern shone in Wright's hand. He choked. His heart was numb with pain. He saw the house clearly, and the barn, and all the farm. It was to have been his, and it could never be his. This was what he had abandoned Amy for. This was what he had driven Amy to distraction for. Amy's master, but the slave of Cricklethwaite's widow.

No Cluff. Cluff not there when he was wanted. Cluff everywhere before and Cluff nowhere now. Cricklethwaite in his grave, witness to the manner of his dying. Ben Crier cold on the kitchen floor. More than Amy in Balaclava Street. The truth about Amy's death no longer relevant. Punishment now for his intent, not for intent transformed into action.

No hope. None. Except in the woman, in the devil she was. No escape without her. None, in the end, with her. Or was there? Could he trust in the power of her evil?

He dragged his carcass by the hay in the barn, through the door at the upper end into the loose-boxes. The farthest box, opening on to the hillside, was a stable. He heard the horse stamping and moving in it.

His larger fear conquered the smaller fear he had of horses. The horse was fastened with a rope from its halter, threaded through an iron ring, prevented from slipping out by a toggle. A horse-collar hung on the wall. Long chains, with hooks at their ends, were festooned on pegs.

The smell of ammonia was strong. The horse's eyes were red in the lantern light. It sidestepped nervously. Its hooves clattered on the paved floor, through the thin covering of bracken.

He took the collar down. He stretched out his arm for the horse. The horse tossed its head. It curled its upper lip and did a little dance with its feet. Wright flattened himself against the whitewashed wall, dirtied where the horse had rubbed, splashed with fragments of manure. Sweat poured on Wright's cheeks. His clothes were clammy. His palms were slippery with moisture.

She said nothing. She pushed past him.

She released the horse. She forced the collar on to the horse's neck. She clipped the hooks on the chains to rings on the collar. She folded the chains loosely over the horse's back.

He went after her with the lantern, on to the hill, where a lean-to was built against the side of the barn.

It was quite dark, moonless, starless, cloud shrouding the night.

CHAPTER XIX

THE SLEDGE WAS SQUARE, A BIG BOX ON IRON-SHOD RUN-ners, for use on the moor, not only in winter in the snow, but in autumn to collect the bracken for bedding, over the short grass.

She completed the harnessing. She led Wright back to the kitchen. They dressed warmly.

"Help me with him," she ordered.

Wordlessly, Wright took Ben's feet and she Ben's shoulders.

They tipped him into the sledge. The horse reared. She snatched its halter and jerked down its head.

"Give me a stick," she said.

Tremors flowed like waves under the horse's skin. Flecks of white foam scattered from its mouth. The woman swore as she struck, in a level voice, using words as foul as any Wright knew.

They wound up the track to the moor. She walked by the horse's head. Wright had his hand on the side of the sledge. The extinguished lantern rattled, nudging Ben's body.

She did not hesitate. Wind from the moortops whipped round them, tugging at their clothing. The horse, subdued, strained, pulling its heart out. The sledge lurched and skidded.

Wright lost all notion of time. They turned from the track over the bracken. The wind moaned like a banshee. Shapes and shadows materialized and vanished without rhyme or reason.

She pulled the horse to a halt. She lifted Ben from the sledge by herself, with no assistance from Wright.

"Bring the lantern," she said.

He followed her, frightened of losing her. They ploughed through the moor growth. They walked on softer ground. Wright's shoes sank in it and this, too, soon ended. He stumbled on hard, smooth rock, inclining upwards.

She stopped so abruptly that he collided with her. She backed against him, her voice tense with warning. Ben's dangling head butted him in the chest. He peered beyond Ben and the rock was cut off sharply. Emptiness stared him in the face. He could not see what was below the sheer face of the rock or how far away it was.

She shrugged Ben from her shoulder into her arms. She drew herself erect. Wright cringed at the intake of her breath as she put forth every ounce of her strength. For a long time there was nothing.

A bump, the heavy thud of something not soft and yet not unyielding. A series of bumps, each less than the one before. He went on hearing them long after they had ceased.

"Light the lantern," she said.

He struck match after match, in the shelter of a boulder, trying to protect the flames from the wind. His hands were too unsteady. She did it for him.

"Take care," she said. "There's a way down, but it's steep."

Her voice was kinder, caressing.

They scrambled down where the crag merged with the moor. The lantern bobbed and dipped.

"I'll stay here," Wright protested at the bottom.

She did not object. The lantern was a pinpoint in the dark, receding. He could see no more of her than her broad side and the bulge of her huge breast, the curve of her hip, a fat thigh moulded under her coat.

He cocked his ears. Her shoes scraped in the loose shale. The light of the lantern steadied.

"You couldn't tell," she said, when she returned, "but that he'd fallen over the crag by accident."

She came closer. The lantern dropped from her hand and went out. Her arms circled round him. Her mouth was groping for his. She moved against him. He was being enfolded in her flabbiness, drowned in her.

Words whispered into his ear.

"In the morning," she murmured, "we'll report him missing. How did we know he hadn't come down from the moor and gone to his cottage in the village without coming in to see us?"

CHAPTER XX

JOHN CLUFF, SURPRISED, ASKED, "YOU'RE NOT FOR THE MOOR again, Caleb?"

"Why not?" Cluff asked.

"The wind's shifting west. It'll rain."

"I'll not melt," Cluff replied.

His brother held a match to his pipe. He sucked and expelled smoke from his mouth. He watched the smoke disintegrate.

"What's wrong, Caleb?" John Cluff asked.

"Nothing I can lay my finger on," Cluff answered slowly. "I have to do the best I can with what there is."

"You'd be better off with me here," John said. "I could get Moor Bottom next door. That place joined to this, we'd be something like. There's a good house and some decent meadows."

"You'll have me married next," Cluff told him.

"It's about time," John said.

"Past time," said Cluff. "Too long past."

"I could find a job on the moor," John offered.

"I'll not be back before dark," Cluff said.

"Suit yourself," his brother replied. "When you're ready you'll tell me about it."

"Maybe."

John stood at the back door watching Cluff and Clive getting smaller in the distance. He turned into the house. His wife was busy with breakfast dishes at the sink.

"What's up with him, Alice?" John asked.

"Leave him alone," Alice told her husband. "He's not here for his health."

A girl of about ten came into the room from upstairs. She had long fair hair and very blue eyes.

Her mother said, "Your father and your uncle have had their breakfasts."

"Where's Uncle Caleb?" the girl asked.

Her father said, "Gone up the moor, Joan."

Joan pouted. "I hoped he'd take me to the bus," she said.

"I will," her father told her.

"I wanted the others to see him," Joan explained. "It isn't everyone who's got a detective for an uncle."

"No," John said. "It isn't."

Alice said, "It's a job like anything else. Worse than some. Better than others." She rattled the dishes. "I'd not like the responsibility on me of deciding what's right and what isn't."

Mist was gathering on the moor. Low cloud wrapped the higher peaks, breaking into a fine drizzle below. Cluff followed the track he had taken on the previous day. He avoided the more sizable ridges but did not descend into the boggy hollows.

Sheepwalks crisscrossed the moor, wide enough for only one animal at a time. He turned from one into another, his sense of direction inbred. He settled down above Ghyll End.

He could not see anyone moving below him. After a while he took a handkerchief from his pocket. It was large and white and he tied it to his walking-stick by two of its corners. He stuck the stick in the ground. The wind took hold of the cloth, holding it stiff and flat.

He sat there, confident that he would be seen sooner or later. He had his hands in the pockets of his coat, his coat collar lifted about his ears. Clive leaned against his leg. The dog's hair shone with a film of wet.

A crowd of men approached Ghyll End up the lane. They congregated at the moor gate. Some of them went into the farm and came out again. They began to climb the moor and Cluff could see them pointing.

He stayed where he was. They came straight towards him, attracted by his makeshift marker. A constable led them. He wore his helmet and a uniform coat, but his trousers were tucked into gumboots. Cluff uprooted his stick. He untied his handkerchief and put it back into his pocket.

"It's you, Symes," Cluff said, as the constable walked to him.

"I heard you'd been in the village," Symes said.

"I'm at Cluff's Head," Cluff told him. "I'm not on duty."

The village policeman hesitated. Cluff did not add to the information he had given.

"Ben Crier's missing," Symes said. "Cricklethwaite's widow came in from Ghyll End this morning to say he'd not turned up for work."

"He was all right the day before yesterday," Cluff said.

"He wasn't in his cottage. It didn't look as if he'd been there all night."

"What makes you think he's up here?"

Symes said, "He was supposed to be gathering sheep yesterday. He didn't bring any down."

"They must have known that at Ghyll End before this morning."

"They?" the constable said. "She didn't look out last night."

"There was no one on the moor yesterday but me," Cluff said.

"It's a big place."

"I'd have seen the dog if I missed the man. I'd have heard something."

"There's nowhere else he can be," Symes said.

"Ghyll End?"

"He's not there."

Symes spoke to his men. They were farmers and labourers, augmented by the village grocer and the postman and the mechanic from what had been the smithy before it became a garage.

"Spread out," Symes told them. "Keep in line."

"I'll come too," Cluff said.

The men worked forward, a hundred yards or so between each, poking with sticks.

Symes said, "He was getting on. It's easy to twist an ankle on the moor, or break a leg."

"Clive," Cluff said. "Seek, lad. Seek! Clive!"

A rock face, flat and high, grew out of the heather. Its base was strewn with loose boulders.

"Call your men in," Cluff said to Symes. "The dog's found something."

Ben was broken over a rock, backwards, his spine shattered. He'd hit the crag face coming down and his head wasn't a pretty sight.

"Where's that stretcher?" Symes shouted.

The man carrying the stretcher ran up and began to unroll it.

"I'll take a look from the top," Symes said.

Cluff wandered about the rocks. They were lifting Ben. He heard someone say, "There wasn't much blood in him. He must have shrivelled up with age."

Symes slid down to them.

"He came over the edge," Symes said. "That much is certain."

"The weather was clear yesterday," Cluff said.

"He was an old man."

"He knew the moor."

"A fit of dizziness perhaps," Symes suggested. "A seizure of some sort."

"So conveniently? Just where he'd fall over?"

Ben was strapped to the stretcher.

Cluff said, "Never mind Doctor Henry. Get a proper pathologist to have a look at him."

"Eh?" Symes exclaimed. "And make an idiot of myself? I'd never live it down. We don't need your clever detective tricks in these parts, Caleb."

The bearers lifted the stretcher. Their companions were beginning to straggle away, grateful that the search was so soon over.

Symes pushed back his helmet and scratched his head.

"He couldn't have lasted much longer," Symes remarked. "He'd had his innings, Ben had."

CHAPTER XXI

THEY'D GONE.

Cluff watched them until they were out of sight. He climbed the course Symes had taken to the top of the crag. He walked over the solid rock slabs and on to the peaty, bare soil beyond. Little depressions in the ground had not sprung back to disappear from view. Cluff knelt and peered at the marks. He visualized the size of Ben Crier and compared his size with the boots he would wear. The disturbances in the peat looked more than one man would make unless he had been wandering round aimlessly in the same narrow compass. Some of them were large enough to fit Ben Crier but there were others, smaller, more sharply defined at the heel.

The Sergeant continued to where the bracken and the heather began. The bracken and heather were too tough and resilient to give much indication of people passing through them. He went in increasing circles, his eyes on the ground. He found a spot where something heavier than a human body had been restless. The bracken was crushed and broken. When he stood back and looked into the distance he could follow a faint double trail across the moor.

"They couldn't get away with it," Cluff thought. "Once they began they couldn't stop. They couldn't walk unseen for ever."

He approached the farm at Ghyll End.

He told himself, "Amy's death wasn't wasted. They were too subtle."

He saw the sledge in the lean-to against the barn. He looked inside it and examined the joins of the boards from which it was constructed. He heard the horse stamping in the loose-box. He tried the door. It wasn't locked.

"Wait for me, Clive," Cluff said and went in.

He ran his hand over the horse, which stood quietly at his touch. He felt the cloth-covered padding on the inside of the horse-collar on the wall. He let the links of the chain harness slip through his fingers and picked out from them fragments of vegetation.

"Not you!" a voice whined.

Cluff turned round. Wright was a statue in the other doorway, the one that led through the remaining loose-boxes to the interior of the barn.

The Sergeant moved forward. Wright, petrified, did not budge. Cluff got hold of Wright by the arm, firmly. He marched Wright into the barn, along by the feed-bins to the big barn door. He was pulling a leaf of the door open when he heard the clatter of buckets.

Cluff dragged Wright between the haymows. He peered down the steps that tunnelled under the flagged platform on which the hay to his left rested. At the bottom a corridor was dusty with hay-seed. The sides of the corridor were worm-eaten planking, chest-high, between upright posts supporting the roof at intervals. The heads of cows poked over the planking, two rows of them facing each other across the corridor. A round, flat bucket, containing cattle cake, was placed under each head. Jinny Cricklethwaite, at the far end of the shippon, began to lift the buckets one by one over the partitions. The cows lowered their heads and ate.

The Sergeant released Wright. He had to bend down at the top of the steps in order to see her properly. So long as he remained erect only his trousers' legs were visible to her.

"They've found Ben," Cluff called loudly.

She dropped the bucket she had in her hands. Its rattle on the floor echoed in the closed shippon. The cows backed, jerking their chains.

Her face looked up at him. From his position above her he could see the deep cleft between her breasts.

Cluff said, "I've seen the sledge and the horse. You don't think they won't be able to tell whether he was dead before he fell?"

"You're clever," she said.

"No," Cluff replied. "There's nothing clever about it."

"What else do you know?" she asked.

"What Ben Crier knew, perhaps. How did Cricklethwaite die?"

Wrinkles appeared about the corners of her eyes and the corners of her mouth.

"You should have left Amy alone," Cluff said.

She began to laugh. Her laugh had a note of hysteria in it. She laughed so hard that tears came to her eyes.

"Do I have to come down to get to you?" Cluff demanded.

She stopped laughing.

"Alf!" she cried. "Alf!"

Cluff's body was inclined forward. A violent push in the back toppled him headfirst down the steps. The stonework on either side of the steps was smooth and his clutching hands found no grip. He bounced awkwardly, half-stunning himself. He lay in a crumpled heap, trying to get up. He lifted his arms to ward off the bucket that was descending on his head. His arms were beaten down. Wright landed on him squarely from above, knock-ing out of him what breath he had left. Wright pummelled and struck him, but Wright's blows were weak and he scarcely felt them.

Cluff bumped unevenly. Hands under his armpits dragged him along, careless of obstructions. Voices murmured indistinctly. A wind was cool on his face and then it faded. He jolted and scraped. His wrists and his ankles burnt and his hands and feet were numb. He got colder. The chill struck at his whole body. His head was splitting. The lids pressed too heavily over his eyes for him to force them open.

He could see again. He could feel. A little window above him admitted a sharp, icy draught. After a while he realized that he was lying against a wall on a stone shelf some distance from a stone floor. His brain began to work. He remembered the pantry he had seen on his first visit to the farm.

He wanted to move, but he could not, not without rolling off the shelf. His arms and legs were lashed together with coarse, strong ropes. The ropes bit at his flesh. He struggled and blood ran warm on his hands. Apart from increasing his pain to a fiery torment he accomplished nothing.

His bonds grew tighter, not looser. His arms and legs were swelling to bursting point. He had to stop and lie still.

He tried to remember more. Little by little the events of the morning came back to him. He remembered the moor. He remembered coming down the moor. He remembered going into the loose-box to the horse.

"Clive," Cluff whispered.

"Clive!" he shouted, more loudly.

He remembered leaving the dog outside the barn in order not to disturb the horse.

"Clive! Clive!" he repeated, afraid for Clive, wondering what they had done to Clive. He pursed his lips and tried to whistle but his mouth was too dry and no sound came.

He could hear nothing. The closed door was thick and solid. His thoughts went round and round in his head.

"Help!" he called. "Help! Help! Help!"

His voice was hoarse and his throat sore. The door opened. She was there, derision on her face. He was ashamed of himself for his weakness.

"What a noise!" the woman said, using the manner she might have adopted to a tiresome child. "I could hear you in the barn, on top of the mow."

He did not answer.

"I'm not Wright," she went on. "You don't scare me just by looking at me."

She came closer. Her face was very near to his.

She said, "What do you expect?"

"Nothing," Cluff replied. "Not after Cricklethwaite. Not after Amy. Not after Ben Crier."

"You can leave Amy out of it," she said. "But the other two are enough.

"You!" she said fiercely. "And Wright! Both of you coming to take from me everything I've planned for."

"It's no use," he said. "You can't get things that way."

She smiled.

"I can only hang once," she told him.

He was alone. He lay quiet.

She was there again. She had a shotgun in one hand, a box of cartridges in the other. She broke the gun. She pulled the lid from the box and took out a cartridge. She inserted it slowly and deliberately into one of the barrels. She loaded the second barrel and snapped the gun closed. She left the safety-catch back and cocked both hammers.

She slashed with a knife at the rope binding his ankles. He rolled into a sitting position on the shelf, his legs touching the floor. His blood forced itself into his feet. He gnawed his lips so as not to cry out. He winced and the pain was intolerable.

She waited, savouring his agony.

"I'm walking behind you," she said. "I'll pull both triggers at the first wrong move you make."

"Why not now?" he asked.

"If you want it that way," she threatened. "Make it easier for yourself and for me."

The gun bored into his back, out of reach of his bound hands. She prodded him out of the front door. He paused on the flagged walk and she let him stand there.

"Take a good look," she said. "It's the last you'll see of it."

The countryside spread before him. The fields were Ghyll End fields. The moor was Ghyll End moor. The lane led nowhere except to Ghyll End.

"No one will come," she said. "I told Symes enough this morning to last him for the rest of the day."

He breathed deeply, filling his lungs with clean air. He blinked to clear his eyes of a mist that was forming over them.

The gun jerked him on.

"Into the barn," she commanded.

He smelt it as soon as he entered. The atmosphere was heavy with the odour of paraffin. He glanced quickly round in an attempt to trace its source. The floor was dry and he couldn't find out where the smell was coming from.

"Alf!" she shouted, in a toneless voice.

Wright came in through the smaller door on the other side of the barn, from the hillside where he had been posted to watch the lane. He closed the door behind him. He was as pale as death. His knees shook and his body trembled. He could hardly stand and he looked as if he was going to collapse at any moment.

They stood, all three of them, between the two mows of hay. A ladder leaned against that nearest to the loose-boxes.

She looked at Wright questioningly. He stammered, "Everything's quiet. I didn't see anyone."

She said, "He can't climb the ladder with his hands tied. Go up first and wait for him at the top."

"Give me the gun," Wright pleaded.

She said roughly, "You couldn't hit him if you tried. I shan't miss from down here."

Wright gripped the ladder, his knuckles white. He put one foot despairingly on the bottom rung.

"The lantern," she told him urgently.

Wright stared at her as if he could not understand.

"By the bins," she said, through clenched teeth.

He went obediently, but it was hard for him. He slipped his wrist through the handle of the lantern. He mounted slowly, hugging himself to the ladder. The sound of his quick breathing came down to Cluff and the woman. Halfway up he stopped. He looked down and shook his head, suddenly giddy.

"Go on! Go on!" Jinny Cricklethwaite shouted.

Wright compelled himself upwards. He threw himself prone on the top of the mow. Only his calves and his feet, in their narrow shoes, were visible from the barn floor.

"Light the lantern," she ordered.

Cluff looked at the hay. It was dry and brittle, three months old. He cringed as a match scraped. A patch of light shone in the darkness between the beams overhead.

"On the hook," she said.

Wright was so close on the hay to the rafters that he did not have to reach up. He hung the lantern to a beam. He twisted round, crouching on his knees, peering between the uprights at the end of the ladder.

"Be quick," Wright mumbled. "Be quick, for God's sake!"

She tugged left-handedly at Cluff's wrists behind his back, whispering warnings, wrenching at the knots. The rope came away. The blood dammed in his arms flowed through veins that had shrunk from lack of it. He flexed his fingers.

She drove him up the ladder, climbing after him. They mounted into a dimness above the shaft of light coming through the main doors of the barn. They emerged into a soft, yellow glow cast by the lantern.

A flat expanse of hay stretched in front of them. It merged level with the flagged floor of a balks that was ceiling to the loose-boxes underneath it. The space beyond the hay was narrow, low. It was strewn with junk, oddments and relics of past methods of farming, their outlines too vague for their nature to be distinguished.

Cluff stepped off the ladder. She pushed him away from the edge with the gun, jumping too quickly on to the hay for him to turn on her.

The hay gave a little under his weight. The smell of paraffin was very strong. Two tins, their tops narrowing into cones, lay where they had been thrown heedlessly. In from the edges the hay was wet in places, its paleness blackened and soaked.

She flung the length of rope she had brought at Wright.

"Tie his hands again," she said.

Cluff knew what they were going to do. He knew that they were going to set the hay alight and leave him on the hay. He knew that there would be nothing left of him to prove that he had ever existed after the holocaust they planned.

Wright stumbled to Cluff. He fumbled behind the Sergeant. The Sergeant flung himself suddenly forward, hurling himself to burrow where the hay joined the balks.

Wright, off-balance, fell flat on his face. He floundered in the soft top-covering of hay.

Jinny Cricklethwaite lifted the gun. She laughed soundlessly. Wright groaned and the woman looked at Wright, not at Cluff.

She did not fire. She tapped the barrels of her gun against the hanging lantern. Its glass cracked. Pieces of glass fell on to the hay. The hay where they rested gave off a faint, blue smoke.

Wright succeeded in gaining his feet. He plunged for Jinny Cricklethwaite, ignoring Cluff. She had the lantern in her hand now. Its flame was naked above the remnants of its globe. The gun she had dropped thudded on the floor below her.

She stepped nimbly on to the ladder. Her breasts overflowed the rungs. Her mirth was audible. She swung the lantern and its flame flickered. She let go of the lantern and it flew at Wright.

Wright screamed. The lantern took him in the chest. Cluff crawled for the stone balks as fast as he could. Wright's terror filled the confined space under the barn roof. A wall of fire leapt up from the hay. It steadied and spread rapidly like water poured from a bucket.

Cluff looked round. He held his hands in front of his face. He took one step towards Wright. Wright was a flaring torch. His screams were uninterrupted, their high-pitched note continuous.

The heat seared Cluff. The ladder he could not reach crashed as the woman knocked it away from the stack. The barn doors creaked and slammed. He knew she had gone.

The fire drove him from the hay to the balks. It was too late to jump. He could not reach the edges of the mow. If he jumped, the twenty feet to hard stone, the least he could expect would be a leg broken. The channel of paraffin that Wright had poured on the hay while Cluff lay in the pantry erupted. It lapped greedily.

Wright stopped screaming. Wright was a black, charred, motionless log, lit by red and yellow and white.

Cluff crouched in the farthest corner, where the flags above the loose-boxes met the angle of the roof joining the rear wall of the barn.

His eyes streamed with the smoke. His lungs were at bursting point. He could hardly see and he could hardly breathe.

He had accomplished what he set out to do. He had exacted from Wright the price of Amy's death.

The cost was high. It included himself.

CHAPTER XXII

THE SCHOOL JOAN CLUFF ATTENDED WAS THREE MILES FROM Cluff's Head.

The bus stopped where the lane from Cluff's Head joined the main road up the dale. John Cluff saw his daughter on to it and waved her off.

He walked quickly back to the farm, as large as his brother, dressed, like his brother, in rough tweed, an identical shapeless, weather-stained hat on his head. He went into his barn. One of his men turned the handle of a turnip-chopping machine steadily. The turnip chips fell clean and orange-coloured on to a sack spread under the machine's mouth. The wheel geared to the revolving blades did not stop. The man continued to turn stolidly.

John Cluff wandered aimlessly about the farm, at this task and that.

Finally he went into the kitchen. He said to his wife, "I'm off up the moor."

Alice nodded. She finished filling the pan with which she was working. She set it on the fire. She went outside. John was climbing the home pastures. She watched him until he was a thin pencil against the grey sky. He vanished below the horizon. Alice stood for a long time, thinking.

John loped easily over the moor, through his own territory. He did not give a glance at the sheep which raised their heads as he passed. He got on to Ghyll End land. He saw something moving on the moor ahead of him. It was coming in a straight, purposeful line, aware of his presence long before he noticed it.

He bent on to one knee and the dog rushed at him. It avoided his grip when he tried to catch it.

"Clive, boy," John said. "Where's Caleb? Where's Caleb, Clive?"

Clive barked frantically. He ran off a little way and stood. He ran back to John and away again.

"Aye, lad. Aye," John said.

He was running himself. He had been a noted fell-racer in his youth. He fixed his eyes on the ground a little in advance of his pounding feet, choosing the places automatically that would not let him down. His coat lay discarded in a heap a long way back. His hat had gone. Clive kept in front of him, adjusting his pace by the sound of John's progress.

They came to the moor edge. The valley spread below them. Ghyll End clung to the slope they were descending. Smoke wreathed through the slates of the Ghyll End barn and through the gaps in the walls under the eaves, like arrow slits, put there for ventilation.

It was not climbing the moors that hindered a man in a hurry, but coming down from them. John leapt from tuft to tuft of coarse grass. He swayed his body to this side and that round the boulders. He jumped to avoid the snaky tendrils of the heather. He landed squarely on the bracken that reached to trip him. He took not the direct course, but the fastest and the safest, exercising all his skill and knowledge.

Clive hardly touched the wall bounding the moor. John went over it too fast for the topstones he brought down behind him to hit him. They skimmed the pastures, the going smooth compared with the moor. They were in the croft at Ghyll End. Hens and geese scattered in panic.

Clive led the way through the wash-kitchen and the dairy. Clive scratched in distraction at the closed doors of the barn, his nose to the gap between their bottom edges and the ground. The flames inside crackled fiercely. They could smell the fire. Smoke blew about them. The air was warm. In the loose-boxes the horse neighed and calves bawled. The cows in the shippon kicked their stalls, skating on the floor slippery with their droppings, calling loudly.

She came up the steps from the shed housing the Land-rover. She jumped on John from the back. Clive went for her, tearing her skirt. She paid no attention to the dog. She clung to John's shoulders, pulling at him, trying to get her fingers on to his neck. He smelt her excitement above the smell of the smoke.

He shrugged his great body, breaking her grip as if she was a child. She fell and slid on the rough surface of the drive along which wagons came to the barn. Her clothes rode high about her thighs. Her stockings gave at the knees, showing calloused skin. Drops of blood began to ooze where the gravel had scraped her flesh. Clive stood over her, forelegs planted on her breasts, snarling. His mouth dripped saliva. His hair lifted in a ridge along his spine. His tail was as stiff as a rod.

John got one leaf of the door open. Flame spurted at him.

She spat, "You're too late, John Cluff. They're in there, both of them."

For a second she thought he was going to kill her. He jumped down the steps. The Land-rover was out of its shed, its nose pointed towards Thorshall. He dashed through the bottom yard. He turned up the slope on the other side of the barn.

The horse appeared suddenly from its loose-box, witless. It went galloping off, over the wall into the lane, along the lane.

The strength went out of John. He staggered.

"Thank God! Thank God!" John muttered.

His brother followed the horse into the open air.

"Caleb! Caleb!" John shouted.

The Sergeant's face was black. His clothes were in tatters. His hair was singed and his fingertips scrabbled raw.

John's voice broke. Clive flashed past him. The dog threw himself on Cluff. The Sergeant fell, rolling, clutching the dog.

"The stock, John," Cluff said.

John wound his handkerchief over his mouth. He fought through the smoke into the end box, where the horse had been. A hole in the ceiling gaped redly. The rafters above the balks were vaguely visible through the hole. The smoke floated against them, ricochetting down. The bedding in the box was piled to one side where Cluff had stumbled as he landed. There were new scratches made by Cluff's boots on the floor. An iron crowbar, rusty, lay where it had fallen after he had prised free his escape route.

The cries of the calves stilled. There was only the roar of the flames. John could do nothing.

Cluff was coming to his feet. John bent to help him. Clive shot away for the bottom of the slope. Cluff's voice halted him. The dog froze, straight-legged, glaring.

Her hair blew in wisps in the wind. Her features were distorted, mottled. Ugly red patches splotched the white background of her face. Her nostrils were distended, her lips drawn back to show her teeth. Her eyes were bloodshot, pin-pointed with hate.

The last button of her grime-matted cardigan parted as she clawed at her throat. She tore at her blouse, stifled, and her breasts were half-naked.

She screamed at them. Her words were a mixture of threats and curses and regrets. Her voice outblasted the noise of the fire. They quailed at the obscenity of her language. She accused Cluff of crimes more than she had committed. She blamed Cluff for the ruin of her hopes, the overthrow of her schemes. She included his brother in her recriminations. She bemoaned the wasted years of her life with Cricklethwaite, the snatching away of the reward she had counted on.

She fled. The engine of the Land-rover whirred into life. The Land-rover burst into the bottom yard. It swerved. Its front wheels slashed into the pile of manure in the open midden. It scraped the gatepost as it drove furiously into the lane. The two men running down the slope saw her crouched over the wheel, with set face and staring eyes.

"God help anyone who gets in her way," John Cluff said.

The roof of the barn fell in. Flames darted into the sky. The smoke was a pall, too thick and heavy for the wind to shift it. A light drizzle had no effect on the fire.

Cluff sat on a wall. He watched the farm burn.

He said, "I had to leave Wright. But he was dead already, before I opened the hole in the balks' floor."

John could not remember who Wright was. He said, "I thought I was too late. I knew you were in trouble. I wasted time making up my mind."

"She's saved us the job of bringing Wright to trial," Cluff said. "I saw his face after she'd flung the lantern. He couldn't believe what she was, and he had to believe it."

The windows of the house cracked with sharp, rifle-like reports.

"Let it all go," Cluff said. "She'll never come back to it."

They set off for the village.

The fire-engine from Gunnarshaw forced them into the ditch, its bell ringing wildly.

They met Symes, sweating like a pig as he pedalled on his bicycle after the engine.

Symes listened to them. Symes said wonderingly, "I didn't know she was as bad as that."

"Go on up there," Cluff instructed. "You'll have to tell them what to look for. Not that there'll be anything of him left."

Symes said, "She was driving like the devil when she passed me."

CHAPTER XXIII

C LUFF USED THE TELEPHONE AT THE "BLACK BULL". HE PUT through a call to Gunnarshaw. He spoke to Mole. Before he rang off Constable Barker interrupted, "You're busier on leave, Sergeant, than ever you were on duty."

He had no car with him and there was nothing to be hired in Thorshall. He cleaned himself up as well as he could. George, the landlord, taped his fingers and the cuts on his head. He sat with his brother by the bar fire in the inn, waiting to hear on the phone what had become of Jinny Cricklethwaite.

George brought large brandies, sugared and topped with water almost at boiling point. Cluff put his hand in his pocket for money to pay for them.

"Damn it, Caleb," George said. "What are you trying to do? Have me up for selling out of hours?"

The rain outside was heavier. A rising wind spattered it on the window panes. George sat down with them and they drew closer to the fire. The winter dusk was earlier because of the heavily clouded sky. Shadows lengthened in the room.

John stirred.

John said, "I'll give Cluff's Head a ring. They'll wonder what's become of us."

He came back into the bar. Cluff looked at his face.

"What's up, John?" Cluff asked.

John lowered himself on to the settle. "It's nothing," he said. "Joan hasn't got back from school yet. Likely she missed the bus."

"I'll try Gunnarshaw," Cluff said. "They ought to have been in touch before now."

Barker said, over the phone, "Sergeant. The Super wants to speak to you. I'm putting you through."

"Hello. Hello," the Superintendent at Gunnarshaw said, "Cluff? Good work, man. Patterson's been in touch from H.Q. We've got an alarm out."

"No news?" Cluff asked.

"She can't get away."

"Hasn't she gone through Gunnarshaw?" Cluff asked.

"She can't have done," the Superintendent replied. "We couldn't have missed her. I'll keep you posted. It's only a matter of time."

The Sergeant put the receiver down. A car stopped in the village somewhere. Cluff stood listening. The car started up after a pause. It came towards the inn and braked. Cluff stamped along the passage and opened the inn door.

A patrolman said, "They told us at Symes's you were here."

The engine of the police car ticked over quietly, its driver alert at the wheel.

"Didn't you meet her?" Cluff said.

"Not a trace of her between this place and Gunnarshaw. We'd have been here sooner but we were keeping our eyes open in case she'd gone through a wall or into a field."

"John," Cluff called.

His brother came out of the bar.

"There's no point in waiting longer," Cluff said. "You've a phone at Cluff's Head."

John looked relieved, as if he was eager to get back home.

The brothers sat in the back of the car, Clive between them, the driver and the patrolman in front. They got to where the Thorshall road and the road up the next dale, in the direction of Cluff's Head, joined, combining into one to continue to Gunnarshaw.

"Left," Cluff instructed.

A school was built a little way past the junction, to serve both dales. The school was unlit and looked deserted. Cluff glanced at his brother, but neither of them spoke.

Headlights gleamed on the road ahead of them, coming their way.

"Stop it," Cluff said.

The police car swung round to block the road. The driver of a single-decked bus brought his vehicle to a screaming halt and leaned out of his cab, his face angry. Cluff got out into the road and walked over to the bus. His brother followed him.

"That's enough of that, Tom," Cluff told the bus driver.

"Sorry," Tom said. "I didn't know who it was."

"Has anything passed you?" Cluff asked. "Either way between here and Daletop?"

Tom considered. "Not so much as a bike," he decided at last.

"Tom," John interrupted. "Didn't Joan get on on your way up?"

"Your wife collected her," Tom said.

"What?"

"What is this?" the driver demanded, concern in his voice. "I picked up the other kids as usual. Your girl was just getting into a Land-rover. It was your wife driving, wasn't it?"

"I haven't got a Land-rover," John said, in flat tones. "You know my car. You've seen it often enough. With the trailer and without it."

"Here," Tom exclaimed. "I wasn't taking much notice. The Land-rover was stopped by the school and it was a woman in it. I thought—"

"Get out of our way," Cluff said.

The car drove fast up the dale. The lights of Cluff's Head shone high up on the hillside to their left.

"Straight on," Cluff told the driver.

"Pull up!" Cluff ordered suddenly.

The driver trod on his brake and looked round, startled. Just behind them, on the opposite side to the farm, a minor road branched off to the moortops.

"Stay here," Cluff told them.

They could hear the quick beat of Cluff's feet through the patter of the rain. Clive whined. The sound of feet ceased. The minutes lengthened. The rain drummed on the roof of the car. It spurted on the road in the light of the headlamps, like tiny fountains. The driver shifted in his seat.

"What the devil's he up to?" the driver inquired.

His companion on the front seat, untalkative, unimaginative, reached inside his coat for a cigarette.

The footsteps began again, rapid, louder, those of a man running.

Cluff emerged from the night.

"Get through on the radio," Cluff said. "Say she's got hold of my niece. I want every man they can spare up here as soon as they can make it."

He turned to his brother.

"I've found the Land-rover," he said.

CHAPTER XXIV

ONCE OUT OF THE YARD AT GHYLL END JINNY CRICKLETHWAITE pressed the accelerator to the floorboards. The seat bucked under her. She tore down the lane and swerved, without slackening speed, for the village. The wind roared into the open-sided cab. Her hair streamed from her head. When she came to the Gunnarshaw junction she turned, without hesitation, away from the town, making for the wilds beyond Daletop.

There were children on the road in front of her, children running from the bleak, stone school by the roadside. A thought struck her and she slowed, scanning the faces of a group of girls waiting under a sign planted in the verge.

The Land-rover stopped.

"Joan," Jinny called. "Joan!"

The voices of the girls stilled. Some of them were pushing one of their number forward, pointing to the Land-rover, saying something to her. The girl came unwillingly.

"Joan Cluff," Jinny Cricklethwaite said. "Come here, Joan."

Joan approached her slowly.

"You know me, Joan," Jinny said. "I'm from Ghyll End."

The child stared at her.

"Get in," Jinny invited. "I'm on my way to your father's. I'll give you a lift. It's better than waiting in the rain for the bus."

"But—" Joan protested, and the bus was already coming along the road, slackening speed to pull up at the stop.

Jinny looked back at the bus. The bus passed the Land-rover and halted. Children climbed in. The bus set off up the dale.

"Come along," Jinny said. "You've missed it anyway."

Jinny moved the shotgun lying on the front seat beside her into the space behind. They started at a crawl, allowing the bus to get farther and farther ahead of them. The bus disappeared over the brow of a rise, between stone walls.

"Your Uncle Caleb came to see me today," the woman said. "And then your father arrived."

She spoke hoarsely and the words stuck in her throat. The child shivered, aware of the woman's torn skirt and the grey knees, gravel-rashed, protruding through holes in her stockings.

"What are you going to Cluff's Head for?" the child asked.

"Never mind," the woman replied. She added, "Ask no questions and you'll be told no lies."

Joan leaned forward, peering through the windscreen into the dusk.

"There," Joan said, breathless. "There!"

She clutched at her companion's arm. Her voice rose. "You've passed it," she accused. "You've passed the turning."

"Let me out," Joan pleaded. She fumbled with the catch on the door. The woman took a hand off the wheel. Fingers gripped Joan's fingers and squeezed painfully.

"Stay still," the woman said.

"Where are you taking me?" Joan said, in a small voice.

Jinny Cricklethwaite stared anxiously at the offside wall, looking for a break in its line. She found what she wanted and branched off the road. They were going up the hillside with Cluff's Head away on the opposite slope. This new road was surfaced with macadam, but very narrow, with a soggy ditch on one side. It climbed straight for the moortops, steep, high-walled, making for the roof of the world. The woman had to release the child. She struggled with the gears.

"No," Joan shouted. "No! I won't! I won't!"

She hurled herself on Jinny Cricklethwaite, clawing and striking, fighting back when Jinny tried to thrust her off, returning to the attack.

The Land-rover left the carriage-way, leaned, recovered, hit a stone wall, rebounded. It came to a jolting stop, its back wheels bogged in the ditch, down which water flowed, its bonnet pointing upwards, its front wheels spinning free. The engine stalled. Jinny Cricklethwaite rained blows on the child's head and shoulders. Joan shrank from her, crying. The woman hit harder and harder, full across Joan's mouth, shouting and cursing. Her hand circled the child's neck, squeezing.

She flung Joan away. The door flew open and the child toppled out into spongy, muddy grass, hitting the ground with a dull thump. Jinny leapt after her and hauled her to her feet.

"I'd kill you," Jinny threatened, "if you weren't going to be useful to me yet. Let them take me if they dare so long as I've got you."

Suddenly, without warning, the woman's hands fell to her sides. She collapsed on to the grass. She squatted on her hunkers, her hands to her face. Joan stood over her, appalled.

"Look what you've done," Jinny Cricklethwaite said, in low, querulous tones. "How are we going to get over the tops now?"

They were going up and up. The woman had the child's hand in hers. The rain was fiercer and colder and gale-driven. The wind dashed at them. Joan moaned, her feet like lead. The woman pulled her along and the child tripped and stumbled, at the point of exhaustion. Jinny's legs dragged. Her strength was going. They were both soaked and battered.

In her free hand Joan clutched a box of cartridges. The gun was icy against Jinny's breast, clasped to her, burning her flesh with the cold touch of its metal barrels.

The ground levelled. The road, faintly luminous, black-shining, wound in a series of curves on the top of the moor. The rain was turning to sleet and whipped them pitilessly.

The black bulk of a road-mender's cottage loomed in the night, dark, silent, crumbling. Ivy was a blanket over its gables and crept to engulf its moss-covered slate roof. Long since abandoned, the ivy held up its walls. Its windows and its single doorway were blocked with courses of brickwork to keep out walkers and tramps, for their own safety, in case the cottage fell down on them if they went inside.

They could go no farther. The child was afraid of the woman and afraid, now, in this emptiness, to leave the woman. She felt her hands free but she could hardly have crawled away, let alone have run.

Jinny Cricklethwaite hammered at the brickwork in the doorway with the butt of her gun. The lintel was low. She could reach the top bricks without difficulty and they fitted loosely. She prised and levered. A brick thudded into the room behind the doorway. A second followed it.

The woman called to Joan. They went through the opening Jinny had made. Jinny felt her way round the walls. What was left of the stairs reached into the blackness at the back, no more now than a rotting, inclined ladder, disappearing into a dark cavity in the floor above. Their shoes powdered plaster that had fallen from the ceiling. Broken ends of wooden slats scratched their arms. The ceiling sagged, like the bottom of a bowl jammed between the cottage walls.

The child groaned in a corner. The woman huddled, nursing her breasts in her hands, consumed with self-pity, on the edge of defeat but not quite over it. She dwelt on her past. Her greatest hate was not for her husband, or for Cluff, or for old Ben Crier, but for Wright. Her one consolation was Wright's death and her part in it. Wright's futility wrung her heart. Wright was the one who had tossed victory away, fleeing, not from what he had done, but from what he had not done, trying to escape, not from Cluff, but from himself.

CHAPTER XXV

S HE LIFTED HER HEAD. THE CHILD MOVED AT HER MOVEMENT. The noises of engines, labouring up the hill, came to them, at first faintly, only an intensification of the wind's whining, then nearer and nearer, beyond the possibility of mistake.

She crept to the doorway. The night was arrowed with shafts of light.

She piled the loose bricks into the opening she had made a little while ago. The more she forced her frozen fingers to action the less she succeeded in making a barricade. The bricks would not stay one on top of another. She gave up her efforts.

She warned the girl, "If you move, or shout, I'll shoot you."

Light flooded through the hole in the blocked doorway. It slid in a moving patch over the rear wall of the cottage, revealing the tottering stairs. It passed and came again, and then a third time and no more.

Jinny Cricklethwaite sighed. Hope made her heart beat faster.

Her heart sank. The cars stopped beyond the cottage. Men were shouting. Engines ground into reverse. The light on the cottage wall reappeared, but steady now, a yellow track across the littered floor.

She lifted the gun, loaded as it had been since she had driven Cluff into the barn with it. She seized the box of cartridges lying beside Joan, wrenching off its lid and stuffing the contents into her blouse. The cartridges piled on the waistband of her skirt.

A man shouted, "Is anyone in there?"

She did not move or reply.

"Give me a torch," a man's voice said. "I'll go in."

"Not you," another voice protested. "Me."

Footsteps approached the door. The woman sidled along the wall, out of the glare of the car headlights. She thrust the muzzle of the gun round the ragged edge of the gap in the brickwork. She pulled one trigger, firing blindly.

Her ears rang with the explosion. The lights went out suddenly. Silence fell.

In the night people were moving again, all round the cottage, unseen. An aeon of time passed.

A voice, very close to the doorway, ordered, "Come out!"

She smiled and pressed her lips tightly together. She felt inside her blouse and loaded the barrel she had fired already.

She fired a second time.

"Now," she heard. "Her gun's empty."

She fired again. Someone drew in his breath so sharply that she heard the sound of it. She reloaded quickly.

"Cluff!" she shouted.

"Turn the lights on again," a man said.

"I'll talk to you, Cluff," she called.

The light came back. She looked round the cottage, at its walled-up windows, at its narrow chimney-opening. She shouted, "There's no way in except by the door."

"Here," she said urgently to Joan.

The child got up and came to her.

"Stand in the light," Jinny said. "A little back from the door."

Joan did as she was told.

She heard the sound of a man struggling in the grip of other men.

"Don't, John," the Sergeant said. "She'll kill you."

"The girl, not her father," Jinny yelled.

His shadow grew on the rear wall.

"That's near enough," Jinny warned.

"What else?" Cluff asked wearily. "This is no fault of Joan's."

"You're her uncle," Jinny said. "Her father's your brother. She's the only child he has. His wife's too old for more."

"You're a devil," he said.

"I've lived with devils," she told him.

He advanced a step. She thumbed back the hammers with a click.

"I can't bargain with you," he said. "I've no power to bargain."

"Don't move," she replied.

"If you harm her," he said, "what good will it do you?"

"No good," she told him. "But what harm will it do you?"

"You're not as evil as that," he said softly.

"For the hurt you've done me," she said, "a hurt in return."

The girl was bedraggled in the light, dirty, wet. Her face was ghostly. She was small and helpless, lost and pathetic. Her eyes were bewildered. She was caught up in a horror she could not understand.

The men about the cottage shuffled. The Sergeant's shadow on the wall did not waver.

Cluff said, "I'm coming in."

His boots squelched rain-soaked earth. His body knocked bricks from the edges of the opening. He had a torch in his hand. He shone it full on Jinny Cricklethwaite. He told Joan, without looking at her:

"Your father's out there. Go to him."

His bulk moved, keeping between the woman and the girl.

"Well," he said, "what's keeping you from shooting me, Jinny?"

Jinny Cricklethwaite sagged. Her arm was too weak to tolerate the weight of the gun. The gun fell from her nerveless fingers.

"You couldn't have shot her," Cluff said.

Emotion had drained out of her. She was empty inside.

"Or me," Cluff added.

She backed away from him, one hand to her lips. He came on deliberately, watching her.

The side of the stairs stopped her progress. He did not halt.

She whirled and sprang up the stairs. He put his foot on the bottom tread and the whole stairs creaked. They trembled. At the top where they were joined to the floor they eased slightly from their anchorage.

She looked down on him.

She said, "I want to make it quite clear. Wright was with me the night his wife died."

He waited.

"He never left the farm," she said. "Whether she killed herself or not, he didn't kill her."

Cluff smiled a little, bitterly.

"You were mistaken from the beginning," she said. "See what you found."

"It makes no difference," he said. "He was no less guilty. He wanted her to die. He drove her to it."

"Yes," she said, agreeing with him. "The drowning of her dog, the way he treated her, they were all directed to that."

"Did you love him?" he asked.

She replied, "He was young. I'd lived too long with my husband. My husband had always been old."

She added, "I wanted him. I thought I wanted him. He was a man. He was handy when the time came."

She glanced about her. The floor here stretched undivided from wall to wall of the cottage, its partitions removed when the last occupants had gone.

She turned away from the stairs and the Sergeant did not call her back.

Cluff remained at the bottom of the stairs. Flakes of plaster dropped from the ceiling as she moved across the space above it. The ceiling shook. It groaned. It hung in a curve more pronounced the nearer she got to its middle.

Laths splintered. The ceiling tore. She came through it in a cloud of dust. She landed with a crash on the stone floor.

Cluff knelt beside her. He wiped the sweat from her forehead with his handkerchief. He smoothed her hair back from her eyes. He pulled her clothes decently across her breasts and straightened her skirt over her shattered legs.

Policemen swarmed about him. They carried her out to the cars. Cluff walked beside her.

She said, "I wanted to kill myself."

CHAPTER XXVI

Annie Croft asked, "Why don't you come round to our house tonight? We can have a game of cards and a bite of supper."

Caleb Cluff shook his head in refusal.

Annie buttoned her coat reluctantly. She tugged at her hat.

"You should have stayed on at Cluff's Head," she said.

"I'd rather be at home," Caleb replied.

"You shouldn't be living on your own," Annie said. "I can't fathom you."

He sat in his chair for a long time after Annie had gone. Jenet purred on his knees. Clive, on the rug in front of the fire, shifted in his sleep.

The Sergeant stared into the flames. It got dark. He lit the oil-lamp.

A letter was propped against a vase on the mantelpiece. Before he sat down again he reached for the letter. The envelope was already open. He read Superintendent Patterson's congratulations a second time. He crumpled envelope and letter in his hand and threw them on the fire, watching them burn.

His head nodded and he dozed, too overcome with lassitude to make the effort of going upstairs to bed.

The telephone rang. Clive stirred. The Sergeant let it ring, not sure that he wasn't back where he'd started from, wondering whether the days between were real.

The telephone went on ringing.

The voice was the same as the voice that had called him out on the night he found Amy Wright dead in Balaclava Street.

"Caleb?" Mole asked, using more familiarity than in the past.

"Are you there?" Mole demanded. "Are you there?"

"I'm here," the Sergeant answered.

Mole coughed.

"You were right about Amy—" Mole began.

"What!" Cluff exclaimed. It was too much to explain, with Wright dead and the affair finished.

"Though if ever a murder looked like suicide—" Mole continued.

"It doesn't matter," Cluff told him.

"You did a good job," Mole said, the words sticking in his throat. "If it hadn't been for you they'd have got away with it. With Cricklethwaite too."

"Is that what you rang me up to say?" Cluff murmured wearily.

"Patterson told me to contact you."

"Well?"

"No doubt of it this time."

"Go on."

"A clear case of murder, thank the Lord."

"Where are you? At the station?"

"Patterson knows you're still on leave. If you don't feel like it—"

Cluff's voice was bitter. "Leave!" he said. "What do I want with leave now?"

Inspector Mole laughed. "It's one of the penalties of having a reputation," he said. His laughter was insincere, with undertones of disappointment and envy.

"You've started something for yourself," Mole added. "It never rains but it pours."

No one answered him.

Inspector Mole's eyes hardened. He slammed the receiver violently into its cradle. He stalked, offended, into the outer office.

"Is he coming?" Constable Barker inquired.

"What the devil!" Mole roared. "I'm not Cluff's keeper. Don't ask me about Cluff. You know him as well as I do."

Also Available by the Same Author

THE METHODS OF SERGEANT CLUFF

It is a wet and windy night in the town of Gunnarshaw, on the edge of the Yorkshire moors. The body of young Jane Trundle, assistant in the chemist's shop, is discovered lying face down on the cobblestones.

Sergeant Caleb Cluff is not a man of many words, and neither does he play by the rules. He may exasperate his superiors, but he has the loyal support of his constable and he is the only CID man in the division. The case is his.

Life in Gunnarshaw is tough, with its people caught up in a rigid network of social conventions. But as Cluff's investigation deepens, Gunnarshaw's veneer of hard-working respectability starts to crumble. Sparse, tense, and moodily evoking the unforgiving landscape, this classic crime novel keeps the reader guessing to the end.

Originally published in 1961, this is the second in the series of Sergeant Cluff detective stories. Televised in the 1960s, they have since been neglected. This new edition is published in the centenary year of the author's birth.

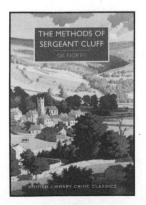

MURDER OF A LADY

Anthony Wynne

Inspector Dundas and gifted amateur sleuth Eustace Hailey tackle a locked-room mystery in a Scottish castle.

DEATH ON THE RIVIERA

John Bude

Counterfeit currency—and murder—darken the sunlit glamour of the Riviera. Detective Inspector Meredith needs to keep one step ahead.

MURDER IN THE MUSEUM

John Rowland

The murder of an academic in the British Museum brings together Inspector Shelley and mild-mannered museum visitor Henry Fairhurst.

THE SECRET OF HIGH ELDERSHAM

Miles Burton

When a pub landlord is stabbed, Detective-Inspector Young calls on "living encyclopedia" Desmond Merrion to help uncover the secrets of the village.